Tower Street, East London, 1975: a crumbling block of artists' studios shaped by the myth of male genius but maintained by Connie, a female caretaker struggling to find her creative voice. Cut to 2017, and this same building is now luxury apartments, the new home of young couple Jane and Tam. Yet their fresh start is jeopardised when a chance discovery brings past secrets to light.

Drawing on interviews with artists, photographers and administrators, as well as autobiographical elements, *Innominate* is a mystery story about privilege and power, in which buildings (and bodies) alternately nurture, trap, and entangle their inhabitants. Perhaps it is only by dissecting the architecture of a place that we can truly understand what happened there.

Naomi Pearce

INNOMINATE

First published in 2023 by MOIST
https://www.moistbooks.com

ISBN: 978-1-913430-14-6

Innominate

adjective

> not named or classified

noun

> either of the two bones forming the sides of the pelvis, consisting of three fused components, the ilium, ischium, and pubis

"Well, what *about* experience? What exactly was it? And where was it? The experience, it seemed, was a large piece of territory. How was she to enter it? From what angle, and in what position? With what strategy, and toward what end?"

Vivian Gornick, *The Situation and the Story*

13 September 1975, the Night

The top deck of the bus smells tired. Stale tobacco, damp clothes. The girl sits gripping the chrome rail of the seat in front, staring at the window's blank expanse, a grey shield of passenger breath clinging to its surface. Smoothing the short pile of the moquette, it's pattern a morse code of orange blocks and blue dashes, she hums the tune of some song; the melody knocks between her ears, reverberates around her skull. She stares at the blood seeping from under her thighs. She thinks about all the other stains she's made. The dull, penny-sized blob on the corner of her mum's apron, its worn cloth pressed to her stubbed toe, aged three. Or just last week, running to the science block—how she'd fallen and made a mess of her knee on the concrete steps. She touches her dress, and afterwards the soft pads of her fingertips stick together as the blood clots. There will be a much bigger stain here now—another place she'll never completely leave.

The sharp points of her knuckles glint in the bright overhead lights. She grips the rail again; her arms begin to shake. *No!* She should be tucked up in bed! *Please*, not like this. It can't be. She's got plans; she's getting away! On to the life of an air hostess, drinking pink champagne, eating escargot. Suntans and water-skis in San Monique. Lovers, travel, more.

She doesn't know what all the fuss is about—the stories of terrible pain. She decides not to look down anymore. Wants everything out. Had he helped her? She can't remember. The memory is a locked room inside her mind. She tries to smile, but no one pays attention; no one sees. *Oh, she has really done it this time!* The other girls won't believe it. Sally will be shocked. She needs to rest… needs to lie down. The lights. She closes her eyes against the glare.

Hairspray and sunshine. She's gripping a trolley—walking down the aisle, the sky all around, cruising at 40,000 feet. The light is sharper than glass. Her lips tremble. She knows God doesn't exist and that this doesn't seem funny anymore. And yet, up here feels like heaven. She looks down at her trolley: stacks of metal trays with tiny spoons and forks; smooth recesses filled with domes of wobbling mousse and rectangular cracker packets. The cabin rocks. Some light turbulence. Nothing to be frightened of, Sir, just a pocket of hot air.

A horn sounds through the clouds; angry toots respond in quick succession. Her eyes flicker, and the smell of hairspray evaporates. Those lights... *Too bright!* She squints; *someone turn off those lights!* She really has done it this time. She hears her mum's voice chiding her, suspicious and disappointed, and bats it away with her sticky hand. Her mouth opens, but nothing comes out. *Terribly sorry.* Sorry for whoever is cleaning tonight. They'll probably have to replace the whole seat. Such an adventure though! Too adventurous this time? It was cold, despite his wool coat. It wasn't his fault. Her dress is ruined, polyester hanging heavy on stockinged legs she doesn't recognise. She feels like a deflated balloon. An itch, now, like she's forgotten something important. Something she'd been taking care of. What was he doing? He was taking care of it. But what about her?

She rocks forward and bumps her head on the rail as the bus shunts along. Where is she now? If she could only get home. A sharp swing right. Playing in these streets since she was little, she knows every curve, every bump. She lifts her head, surprised as she does so by its weight. She wipes the window with a cold hand, the darkness revealing only the reflection of a dishevelled girl with matted hair.

Bethnal Green Road. "My stop," she murmurs, reaching for the bell cord with a lumpish hand but only grasping air. She hasn't been quick enough; it's caught up to her. A slap of cold linoleum on her cheek. If she can just rest here for a few minutes. She shuts her eyes, then tries to open them again but she's so tired. Why is her pillow so gritty? The seats are the wrong way round, upside down. This must be what it's like for those astronauts. An old woman's face with joined-up wrinkles comes into view. She looks scared, her lips moving but with no sound coming out. *Why can't I hear her?* Terror flashes through her, a cold sharp bolt from her head to her guts, then disappears as quickly as it came, and she doesn't care about the seat's pattern or the state of her dress. Her limbs are numb, plucked like petals from a daisy. The trouble is here. As the last breath leaves her body, she's cruising at 40,000 feet and the world of dresses and mums and bus seats with bloody puddles doesn't matter up here.

Bone is built of two basic components: flexible fibres of collagen and brittle chains of calcium-rich mineral hydroxyapatite. These relatively simple ingredients, the springy and the salty, are woven together in a complex web of interlocking layers. The result: an engineering feat of tensile, compressive and elastic strength.

8 April 2017

The fields fan from the building's waist like an A-line skirt, its lush green panels divided by seams of cycle lanes and gravel paths. "Tower Street is a fusion of heritage and contemporary influences" the listing had said, "standing on this East London Street for more than two hundred years" and now part of the local area's "ongoing renaissance". We'd cringed at the hyperbole, but the listing did its work on us anyway. Do buildings really stand? Perhaps, like people, they settle. Bricks sinking into mortar over time.

The scale of our new home will take some getting used to, stark echoing corridors intended for proper industry: grimy fingernails, tinnitus, black snot. According to the developer's brochure, Hackney was full of rag trade, Jewish immigrants, textile producers, men's suits and women's stockings. The building had once been dense with bodies, a single workforce toiling together. Now it holds mostly couples and single professional occupants atomised in partitioned cells. During the viewing, the agent pointed out repeated indentations in the concrete floor, the weight of cast iron table legs, stamped like pores into the building's skin. No handsome sightlines to admire from an armchair. No bespoke wallpaper, or trailing plants hanging from macramé rope holders. No sitting at all in fact, except for at sewing machines.

"Come on, stop daydreaming, we've got to get the van back by four."

Jane moves me to one side by my hips and reaches into the gloom for more of our belongings.

"Yeah, yeah, I know, sorry. It's just, it's happening."

"Ah, how sweet," she says and pecks me on the lips before hoisting a box labelled "Bathroom" up to her chest.

15

I taste her sweat, the sour tang of last night's beer.

"It's happening alright." She smiles, squinting into the spring sun.

We'd not been looking long before finding Tower Street, so weekend viewings still felt novel, asking ourselves: what kind of people are we? Not just now, but in twenty years? Every Saturday trying on a different future. On weekday evenings, as I waited for Jane to finish her shift at the restaurant, I watched reality TV compulsively, *Homes Under the Hammer* and *Location, Location, Location*. I smirked as Kirsty and Phil press-ganged awkward newlyweds into buying an end-of-terrace house in Argyll and Bute, or a family of five buy a semi just outside the M25. Now I understand their stunned expressions. Is this really where I'm meant to be?

And yet, as we'd left the overground that morning last June, turning right and passing through the railway arch furred with emerald moss, I'd got a feeling straight away. *The* feeling. This was it. The fields, the lido, sun dappling against brick, railings peeling, hand-painted street signs buttressed against shiny metal ones. New and old together and the building's façade, unchanged, a backdrop to it all. One year on and we are finally doing it. We've persevered, survived the development's delays, the sceptical friends and their repetitive questions, the anxious parents wringing hands, bank managers with ultimatums. We'd almost lost the mortgage; Jane had started to get cold feet. I'd dug in, I'd said, trust me, and to her credit, she had.

I shift Jane's battered toolbox out of the way and gather two suit carrier bags stuffed with shirts and dresses I've not worn in years. It's best not to touch her things; I'll only break something, and today we're both trying to be calm. She's already halfway across the road and I jog to catch up, the bags getting caught awkwardly between my knees. I'm not built like Jane; I lack coordination. From behind, the muscle between her index finger and thumb bulges as it crushes into the side of the cardboard box. A prickle of excitement needles my spine. I noticed this muscle the first time we talked, saw it pulse with blood as her hands fidgeted nervously with her drink. She saw me looking and felt the need to explain. As she talked knife skills and chef work, I felt my cheeks get hot. Months later, once we'd become sufficiently entwined, I kneaded the muscle gently between my teeth and asked if I could eat it fried with butter like a plump little scallop.

We're on the second staircase and starting to shuffle. The bottles of toiletries jangle loudly against some electronic weighing scales and an old hair dryer. There are still so many more boxes to shift. If only she'd let us pay for someone.

"Did you go through everything before you packed?" she asks.

"Yeah," I lie.

"Because you didn't use half the stuff in that cabinet."

"Not true." I lie again.

I picture the tubs of denatured vitamin C serum, dusty cans of hairspray and half full bottles of moisturiser. She grunts, and readjusts her grip, irritation palpable. In the early days things were different. One night, I'd caught her unscrewing tubes and sniffing bottles, searching for the source of my smell.

As we reach the top step, the bottom of the box collapses.

"Fuck!" shouts Jane, scrabbling to catch the falling contents as they scatter across the floor.

"Shit." I drop the clothes and rush towards her.

"What did I tell you!"

Our heads bump as we reach for the same broken bottle of retinol, its pale-yellow liquid oozing onto the floor's polished concrete.

"Leave it" she says through gritted teeth.

"Well, if you'd let me book a removals company."

She looks furtively down the corridor. "I'm the one doing all the hauling, aren't I," she says and gestures at my sad crumple of clothes on the stairs below. "If you'd only packed things properly."

I say nothing, walking instead towards the tub of conditioner rolling down the corridor. Jane grabs a flannel from the collapsed box and scoops up the retinol in two perfunctory swipes, like she's cleaning the kitchen counter after service. I stand over her, watching blankly. I'd underestimated how packing up all this crap would make me feel. Little pots of memories now thriving with bacteria. Jane's right, why didn't I just get rid of them? What was I holding onto?

The landing is freshly painted. Everything sprayed bright and white. In the flat down the corridor a radio plays. I smell toast and coffee. We stand in silence for a few seconds as though we've forgotten how we got here. Jane looks at me expectantly. I say, "You've got the keys."

I'm glad we don't have much stuff, because despite the building's appearance of scale, truth is, the flat's fucking tiny. It's just under 1,000 square foot with an open-plan layout, pitched roof and one mezzanine bedroom. Massive windows though. I love how they sweep along the full length of one wall. Rectangular panes set within large steel frames opening outwards from a hinged central point. Elegant. On our first visit, when everything was still raw cable ends, rubble sacks and capped pipes, I'd felt unnerved by their easy tilt, the long drop. But on a day like today, with the sun, wow, we are so lucky to get windows overlooking the fields.

"Can you imagine not seeing the fields?" Jane says.

"I was just thinking that!" I take the olive branch. We can still find each other.

"They really make it, you know?" She smiles and adds the tool box to the pile in the middle of the floor and adjusts her belt. The buckle digs into the soft folds of her belly.

I drop the suit bags on the floor and pace around; it's only the second time we've seen everything complete. The ceiling seems lower than I remember. We've got to put our stamp on it, like Kirsty and Phil say. The floor is original. They've done a good job of restoration. It's a shame they didn't keep the exposed brickwork: just one wall in the kitchen would have been enough. Maybe that'll be our little intervention, a project we can work on together.

"Do the ceilings seem lower to you?" Jane doesn't respond so I continue. "I like the kitchen island. I didn't think I would, but it's actually good quality granite." She's looking at her phone, frowning and tapping furiously. The worktop is smooth, cold. I imagine resting my forehead on it in the summer after a sweaty run in the park. "We've got this whole double aspect thing going on. Which is good because of my SAD. We can put the lamp there; the chair can go here. I'm finally going to get that armchair reupholstered. Can't believe how the sun has bleached the old fabric. Need to decide the paint colours first. Tonal could work."

Jane doesn't look up; I stop and stare at her, folding my arms tightly so she can't see my clenched fists.

"Jane."

"Sorry, it's work, one sec." The frown lines in her forehead deepen.

"They know you're moving today, right?"

"Uh huh. It's just… Hamid is sick."

"It's our first night here." My chest tightens. I pull myself up onto the granite. Goose pimples ripple across my bare thighs as the thin fabric of my sundress rides up.

"I'm trying to sort it." She chews the inside of her cheek.

19

I look out at the tips of the plane trees, branches beginning to bud. Jane's restaurant is on the other side of the fields, part of why we'd chosen this place, so she can walk to work. It suddenly strikes me our proximity might allow for something else: escape.

"I can't just leave them to it. You know how it is. People need to eat…" She lets out a long sigh and her shoulders cave. I know she means it, that there is nothing I can say to persuade her. Resigned, I wave her over, and she submits, head bowed. She holds me stiffly at first, but then, as I stroke the soft stubble of her hairline she relents. The full weight of her body transferring onto mine.

"I'm sorry," she murmurs, breath hot against my neck. "I'll be back as soon as service is done, I promise." The cold ridge of her belt buckle presses into my underwear; I feel her pelvis tilt upwards, and I wrap my legs around her as the muscles in my groin contract.

We didn't see the place until they started the redevelopment. The factory closed at some point in the late sixties, becoming an artist studio for a time, before lying empty for ten years, stuck in probate. Much like bodies, buildings decompose quickly when unoccupied. How bad had this one got? I saw my first ruin when I was thirteen, and I never forgot it. Cassandra's birthday party. Marilyn Monroe mole on her cheek, eyebrows plucked into matchsticks. We were walking through wet green fields. In the distance, a dusty sandstone manor with pillars. How it loomed over us as we breathed hard through nervous giggles. A low window, plywood shutter rotted loose, easy; we were only small. Inside, waves of sickness as though with vertigo: a grand ballroom, the ornate ceiling black with mould, the floor a thick carpet of rotting leaves. My reaction was physical. Nausea. Witnessing something once so valuable abandoned, left to fail.

A month later

Step number one, adjust the light and contrast. You need to work in layers: good layer organisation means you won't get lost in your image. I'm trying to get rid of all the little things disturbing the eye—the blemishes which break the harmony of an arrangement. There are some general principles no matter what you're touching up—a car, a bao bun, someone's face. Yesterday was a hybrid mattress feature, today a plate of fresh pesto with some avocado and basil on the side. With food, it's got to look tasty of course, but there's also a certain level of comfort you're trying to elicit in your viewer. Let's be honest: we're all buying to be soothed. I'm no better, I can't stop hoarding skincare. Despite the bottles broken during the move, our new bathroom cabinet is already full. It's about textures. I like the sensation of creams, serums and powders. That's why Photoshop is such a strange tool—it's trying to recreate a feeling without any materiality. It's sort of perverse if you think about it, spending your day simulating feeling.

After about forty minutes of work, I get restless. I've tried everything to help me concentrate, but it's always the same. My focus slides anywhere but the screen. Today, it's that pile of half empty cardboard boxes in the corner. Jane had been right. Whatever they contained, I don't miss it. We unpacked most of our belongings quickly, needing things; where is the loofah, have you seen my crocs? The remaining boxes hold the miscellaneous materials we've collected these last few years. Shared things. Things with limited sentimental value, useless junk, but I can't let them go. Like our bed, they give the impression of togetherness. A high-pitched scream in the street below makes me jump.

"Evie, stop. Evie!" The woman's voice: sharp and desperate. I crane my neck towards to the open window and watch as a child is scooped up from the road kicking and squealing.

"Remember we only cross with mummy."

It's unnerving how sound travels up here. The redevelopers clearly never thought about acoustics. The windows catch voices like an ear. Whole conversations reach me, crystal clear, tales of domestic irritation and big city dreams, young hustlers and former hustlers intersect and meander, each oblivious to the other. Sounds. They're everywhere. It takes all my willpower not to investigate every creak or gurgle. Jane says I just need time to get used to it, the Victorian plumbing, the eerie emptiness of the park in the early hours. Everything becomes familiar eventually. But there was something else, I'd tried to explain it to her, a rhythmic presence like breath, barely a sound, more like pressure. I feel it on my stomach in bed, a weight. The hairs on my neck stand on end. She still doesn't believe me. What would she know? Never here long enough to notice, always antsy to get back to the restaurant. It's lonely. I miss having colleagues. I don't think it's good for me to spend so much time alone. Four days since I left the flat, four days listening to the chatter of other people's lives. It's alright for Jane. She's got a schedule. Lunch and dinner, like clockwork.

I send the same message to five contacts. *Hey! Any plans this afternoon? Be nice to catch up if you're free xx.* Let's see who replies. Maybe I'm hungry. 10:45, too early to eat. Dehydrated? I put the radio on. (Each morning I try and do an hour in silence. My current record is twenty minutes.) It's time to stretch. I stand up, sit down, refocus. The image is starting to come together now that rogue basil leaf has gone. It was disturbing the flow. Last stage: colour correction. I click and select a solid colour. I'll put this on top of that layer. I want to make the greens greener so I'm going to select the greenest green I possibly can. I want it to be super, super bright: I can

22

tone it down later. The main thing is the avocado, dollop of pesto and bunch of basil all look like they belong together. Cohesion is key.

Food isn't my favourite thing to retouch—I prefer people. They appreciate the results. Although, I guess I have a plate of orecchiette to thank for my life now. Glossy ricotta and wilted spinach, her fingerprints still visible in the delicate surface of each piece of pasta. As I lifted the highlights and made the reds of some adjacent cherry tomatoes pop, spit pooled in my mouth. When the weekend supplement came out, I found myself reading the full article about this hot new chef who was transforming East London's restaurant scene. I wanted to meet the woman who made this food.

In the restaurant she didn't disappoint. I sat at the orange Formica bar in my leather pistol boots, chunk of a black heel hooked over the stool's footrest. I watched her work. Saucepans leveraged in flame, hot oil spitting, juicy steaks thinly sliced by sharp blades. I knew she could sense me looking but her shy eyes refused to reciprocate. Quick, controlled movements: quiet, focussed. The way she rubbed her thick forearms and yet delicately drizzled honey from a spoon. Her line cooks were attentive to the slightest eyebrow twitch or pursing of her thin lips. I wanted to taste everything. So, I kept coming. In hindsight, this boldness was unlike me, and even now, I can't tell you why I acted this way. Eventually, one night, Jane broke. I'd timed it perfectly, a late sitting on a Wednesday night. Service was over, only a few tables remained: single workers not wanting to go home and first dates not sure of who's home to go to. She walked to my end of the bar to make a drink, picking her way through rum and vodka and lifting out a green bottle of mezcal with a handwritten label. I stared at the back of her neck, admiring the rectangular shape of her head. I complimented her polenta cake—not a particularly original move, but it was enough. The room dissolved into a blur of moving chefs' whites as the staff sprayed and wiped surfaces, both of us unaware of the descending hush. Locked in. She nursed her small tumbler and asked me questions, so many questions. Who are you? Where are you from? Why do you keep eating alone in my restaurant? My insides liquified when she looked at me, as though her gaze were an electric current.

The news comes on the radio, and I turn it off. One month since we arrived, and I feel worse, not better. Spent a year waiting for this flat, never thought about what we'd do when we got here. Everything in the fields is blooming. Flowers, leaves, birds even. Life surging. Why do I feel so flat? Like I'm doing the opposite, sinking into the soil, going further underground.

My phone beeps. *Tam!! Can't wait to hear about the new place. We're walking the dog later, could meet you in the park at 4?* A message from Fi, an old colleague. We haven't seen each other in months. At least Fi and her uninspiring husband Charles like to chat, so I won't need to contribute much. I can always just play with their dog. Act happy, be happy, right? I uncross my legs and put both feet on the floor. I breathe in and out. Tonight, I'll try. Me and Jane will find each other again. She'll make my favourite tea: fishfinger sandwich, with thick slices of tomato and caper mayo. I'll get baclava. Sweet and sticky. My hair will be washed and blow-dried. My skin will be moisturised. I'll be warm and charming, slightly tipsy but not too much. I'll let her talk about work. I'll listen. Everything will be fine.

Later that day

My fingers stink of garlic. Thick waterlogged aubergines shine in the sun. Soil-caked carrots, fresh. Terry the greengrocer looks happy to see me. He's an old boy with a kind face. I dig into a bucket of Aleppo peppers. I can't get enough of these puppies, gnarled like old witch fingers - slightly oily flavour, medium heat. All the way from Syria. Perfect as a marinade for halibut with a bit of lemon juice. Ceviche style. In the restaurant we serve the fish with wafer thin slices of red onion and sumac. The sharp contrast of tangy, smoky spice with oily citrus fish: magic. The tomatoes are past their best, but this is how Tam likes them. A little bit of give in the flesh means more flavour. I'm cooking, aren't I? She'll appreciate that. It's normal for chefs not to cook much at home. Food is my world, but it's something I associate with a certain level of performance. I don't want to be performing at home. Besides, I shouldn't have to.

A summer haze is setting in, heavy. That special light. Flies are darting around pints with the same frantic energy as the students holding them, everything glinting in the sun. I rarely have Saturday night off, so I don't usually see the street like this. Matching floral dresses spill from the pub. A cloud of vanilla. Go on, roll towards the fields; sleep off day-drinking before the night begins. What would I know? I never went to uni; I've been working in kitchens since I was fifteen. The girls link their golden freckled arms. The market's winding down, but all day it's been pumping. Quality meat, olives and antipasti, French cheeses. Not just food either: bespoke stationery, handmade wooden toys, upcycled furniture. Overpriced like everything these days. Two women, red beaks and violet curls, local accents. Most of the people at the market are newcomers like us; it's a shame, but then such is life, things change. We are part of the problem. I can't do anything about that; I focus on what I can do, on making sure I've got good people in the kitchen, ones who have worked for it. I said to the owner, a public schoolboy with designs on being a famous restaurateur: I build my own team and choose the menu, no questions asked. Take it or leave it. It was just after *The Times* article came out and the phone was ringing off the hook. He couldn't say no. I reach the end of the market and stop on the corner by the newsagents. I'm not ready to go home: it's too nice out.

At the restaurant we concentrate on ingredients, putting good things together with care. Unfussy food. No gels or foams on my menu. Taste is what matters. Our food is simple but not basic. Seasonal, of course. I'm a cook, not a chef. That's what we do. I want the restaurant to be somewhere people want to eat in, sure, but I want it to be the kind of place young chefs want to work too. I spent too long doing double shifts for shit bosses. You lose your creativity, so it's totally unproductive. I work my team hard, but they know how much it means to me.

The corner shop's been here over thirty years. They've seen so much come and go; I make sure I buy something every time I pass on my way home. A paper, a can of beer or a scratch card. In the early hours, after a long shift, I decompress in the fields. Just the dew and a few rough sleepers. Mostly I sit alone on a bench and drink my beer. Sometimes they'll talk to me, and I give them a few quid. Never had any trouble. Usually we keep a respectful distance, aware of each other's presence. We're both just passing through. I think there's a kind of unspoken agreement - either they know the dawn worker is off limits or the fields are a kind of backstage for both of us. Even bums have got to take a rest from begging. They'll be grinding and grafting now that's for sure. Too much money and middle-class guilt about.

Burning sausages on disposable foil BBQs; cigarette smoke and butterscotch vape. The ticker tape of bicycle chains, boom box beats. Slacklines strung up, frisbees thrown. Dog shit and melted ice cream. Babies crying by the tennis courts. "'Bout time," a woman with lime yellow nail extensions says as she takes a call, swiping at the screen with a talon before peeling herself from the bench. I take her spot, crack my can and check my watch as the yeasty bubbles shoot through my nostrils. 5:30. Tam won't mind if I'm a bit late. Two guys in tight shorts on a woollen blanket with rust-coloured stripes. A pale slender leg wraps itself around a deep brown muscular one. I take another swig.

Opposite the bench, the lido queue stretches around the fence and into the gravel path. Frustrated tuts and moans as a trickle of wet heads dawdle from the exit. A femme with stick-and-poke tattoos scaling her thighs, glances over, her gaze lingering for a moment. I lick my lips instinctively and she bottles it, reverting back to her book. Nice day for a swim if that's your thing. Tam likes to swim; she's good at it too, graceful in the water. Her family have a pool. We had sex in it one night, our bodies glowing under the water. She bit my lip so hard when she came it bled. Droplets swirling around us like trails of red smoke. I think the idea of getting caught turned her on.

A raft of clouds darkens the sky. Wind's picking up. Sunbathers with oily pink backs reach for discarded T-shirts, wincing as they move burnt limbs. I try to release the tension in my neck, and vertebrae crunch as my head rotates. Maybe I'll have a bath before dinner. The tarmac path leading all the way home stretches in front of me. We need to get moving with DIY, before things get too bedded in. Tam seems to have lost interest in making any changes, despite the fact she was the one who wanted to expose the brick wall in the kitchen. Why watch all those interior design shows if you're not going to do anything? I know it's messy, but it'll be worth it. It'll look banging. I've got to do something.

Prams, Spanish exchange students, rollerbladers gliding by. I stop briefly at a confluence of cycle paths and desire lines, small unofficial footpaths, dusty tracks scored in the sun-baked grass, at odds with the park's plan. Two collared doves bob past, their necks' pale feathers split by twinning dashes of black.

"Gooose, goosey goo goo!"

Her voice is high and shrill, babyish. I spin around and duck behind a tree. My chest tightens. Tam is about a hundred meters away, her face flushed, obscured, her blond hair scraped back into a messy bun. It needs a wash.

"Are we playing?"

The dog is one of those small breeds—dark brown, fluffy. I guess a poodle or a spaniel: I don't know dogs. The animal is scooched down on its hind legs, jaw to the sky, one end of a stick in its mouth, the other in Tam's hand. They're tussling in a small patch of grass. In the commotion, the tote bag over her shoulder comes loose and the contents falls onto the ground. She's always got so much shit in there. A man and woman I don't recognise stand nearby, smiling. Tam has a lot of so-called friends. Superficial relationships. They never see her like I do. The woman wears a pair of distressed mum jeans with her choppy fringe, while he is bearded in a white tee and khakis. All straights look the same. Tam grabs the dog's head with both hands, rubbing its ears with clumsy hard strokes. I feel the urge to run the other way. What's wrong with me?

"You're such a cutie. Oh, she's super, super cute."

I hate that word, super—super this super that. I ban it in my kitchen. It sounds so insincere. I hang back, use the tree for cover. From here, I see her differently. Properly. Like other people see her: the face she wants to show the world. She looks happy. Really happy in fact, you'd never know. So much happier than she looked at home this morning.

If I keep walking and go the normal way back, I'll have to talk to them. My chest is actually hurting now. Like I can't breathe. I don't want to talk to them. I shouldn't have to. They're not my friends. I don't even like dogs. I turn quickly and head back towards the lido. Tam would understand; it's nothing personal, I've just had a long day.

The image of bone as permanent, like a skeleton forever stuck in a cupboard, has created a false impression. Once formed, bones change. Osteoblasts secrete new bone, laying it down like bricks, while osteoclasts dissolve old bone tissue: a cellular demolition crew. What occurs is an ongoing process of replacement; this bone remodelling is occurring constantly within us. It is happening right now.

5 January 1975

A three-and-a-half-tonne truck accelerates into a set of steel gates. Hunched in the driver's seat is a big man in a flat cap; his liver-spotted hands grip the steering wheel as his boot stomps on the pedal. Out in the street, hiding in the shadows, a younger lad beckons him forwards, vibrating with lean muscles. As truck meets gate the clash of metal breaks the quiet darkness of London Fields.

"Almost, almost! Hit it again!" the lad spits, sweating despite the cold.

The truck reverses: the clutch crunches, rubber skids. And then forward it goes again. Still the gate holds like a pair of pursed lips. The big man says nothing. The firm set of his mouth is hidden by coarse white bristles, tips yellowed from years of pipe smoke. The truck, like the other vehicles in his care, seems part of him. They are what settled people might call his home, in the absence of bricks and mortar.

Since their last visit British Rail had reinforced the gate with a steel plate. He's dealt with things like this before, but tonight, he's tired. It's becoming harder and harder to exist like they used to. Can't just pull your trailer up for a time and then move on. Hassle everywhere. He's getting too old. One more go. The muscle at the corner of his bristled cheek pulses, and breath fogs up the windscreen as he rams into the metal. The gates sway mockingly, as though being tickled by a breeze. No use. Have to try another way.

Metres from the truck, sleeping in a damp room on the ground floor of a former factory, Connie's eyes snap open. The tip of her nose pokes from under heavy wool blankets, a storm of coarse black hair rages across the pillow. For a moment she waits, eyes blinking, stiff in the burrow of the single bed. Another crash rattles the windows. Bollocks. There it is again. Her heart thumps. She sits bolt upright. Underneath the covers, wiry limbs agitate into action. Connie is twenty-two, but often mistaken for much younger, her small frame nimble and quick. Danger, but where? She shuts her eyes, straining to locate the sound's source. She imagines the makeshift warren of artist studios stretching out behind her. It could be coming from anywhere. The building distorts sound, something the previous caretaker, Harold, had warned Connie about, but which, being newly appointed, Connie is only beginning to understand.

She stands rigid, shivering in moth-eaten long johns. It's coming from the street. An engine running. Chugging diesel. She reaches for the clock balanced on the upturned fruit crate by her bed. Peering at the slowly ticking hands, the time reads 3:45. A flash as a vehicle drives past, its headlights illuminating the sparsely furnished room for an instant, remnants of last night's saveloy and chips still on the table. Silence. Connie edges slowly towards the window, nudging her face through a slit in the curtains. Two figures pass quickly, their shadows moving across her body. She licks her chapped lips and holds her breath. They walk with purpose towards the gate of the empty railway yard next door. A dog slinking softly behind them. The glare of a sodium light stretching above her window casts a queasy yolk across the scene. A fist thumps on the door.

"Fuck!" She grips her chest.

"Connie, you awake?" The man's voice is excited. Jim. Of course. The banging continues.

"Shhhh. Alright, I'm coming!" She grabs her keys from a hook by the door and opens it. He hovers on the threshold, skinny and eager, his eyes—as always—moving like roving hands.

"Tinkers!"

"What?"

"Gypsies."

"And?"

"Oh, give over. I've called the police," Jim says, almost salivating.

"Why? What do they want?"

"What do you think Gypsies want? You see that bloody truck? They're moving in! Thought the whole wall was going with it." As he speaks, his voice catches in the flapping folds of his throat.

"It's four in the bloody morning, Jim. Besides, that yard hasn't got anything to do with us." She doesn't want to give him the satisfaction of being right.

"Management won't like it. No way. And it'll be on your head…"

Connie sighs. He has a point. "What they doing now?"

"They've got bolt cutters. Come on, there's a better view from my floor."

Connie grabs a winter coat from behind the door and stamps her feet into boots stiff with cold. Jim is pacing the courtyard outside, two fingers twiddling the thin black hair of his crown. He has a nose for other people's business: he's the first to complain at meetings, but the last to offer anyone help. As caretaker of the artists' studios, she's learnt about his habits: how he likes to sweep the corridors, or try and trap you in long, meandering conversations about the whereabouts of the Red Army Faction. Judging by the cheques she's processed in the office, a wealthy aunt still pays his rent. Typical. He was one of the first artists to move into the building three years ago and careened around the premises with an irritating sense of ownership. Connie's caretaking job doesn't really pay, but it lets her live in the building rent-free. Situated by the factory's entrance, her flat is a squat two-storey brick structure which acts as a buffer between the street and the studios. Officially she's the only one allowed to live onsite and although a few artists break the rules, Jim does it flagrantly, roaming the corridors at all hours. Everyone at Tower Street seems to have built up an

33

immunity to him—something she hopes to develop quickly. He gets under her skin, but for once she's glad of Jim's company. Connie doesn't like to walk around alone at night. The building is a series of interlinked brick warehouses clustered around a small central courtyard. One façade overlooks a dark and deserted London Fields, the other runs parallel to the railway line, itself flanked by empty yards and soggy arches. The wider area is a dusty bomb site, old industry clinging on, rubble and dampness, grim corners.

They make their way towards the back staircase, passing through the courtyard into the main building and along the ground floor. All is quiet. Jim scampers quickly in front of her. They climb two flights, reaching a small landing with a window. Three doors lead into clusters of partitioned studios. The window overlooks the railway yard next door and, despite the darkness, Connie makes out the shadowy figures of both men through the gaps in the metal gate below. Jim disappears into his studio through the first of the three doors.

In the street, the big man fumbles with a long-handled pair of bolt cutters under his jacket. The lad wrangles with the chain, positioning it, holding it still as he crouches low. Their gloved hands moving awkwardly. Shitting hell, it's cold. The dog stands alert, its long face turning sharply between them, ears pinned back, a low growl squeezing from its jaw. The men, so engrossed in their act, do not hear the Black Maria, engine quiet, rolling slowly around the corner. The dog senses danger before they do, turning to look for the source. No sirens, no fanfare. The dog barks. Just once, sharply. The men freeze. "Coppers. Away!" But it's too late—they're on them.

Connie watches as the lad shoots up like a rocket. The clang of dropped tools, the muffled wrestling of thick jackets. Shouts and scuffles in the gloom. A twist of bodies and there, caught in the white beam of a police torch, the boy's long limbs scrambling up the fence. Good on him. Wait. He's not going over. Shit. Higher. From the fence towards the studios, clinging as though his hands secreted glue. Shit. Palms on the flat asphalt roof of the building's single storey section. Shit. Heaving himself up, his chest and his arms pumping. She swears he's laughing at his own fight. On. Running. Shit. Out of view. Shit. He's going up again. The caretaker's flat. Shit. He's on her roof.

Suddenly Jim reappears, a milk bottle of yellow liquid in his hand.

"What did I miss?" he says breathlessly, accompanied by a slosh from the bottle.

"He's on the roof," she sighs.

"Bloody cheek of 'em!"

"Jim, is that a bottle of piss?"

He taps his nose. "Well, if they will insist on trespassing." He licks his lips.

In the street below, police radios crackle, interrupted by grunts from the old man as he's jostled into the police car. Connie and Jim stand in silence, listening for the sound of the lad's footsteps on the roof.

"Bloody nuisance. This'll teach him," he says, gesturing at the bottle.

Connie grimaces. "Maybe it's best you stay out of it."

"I'm not letting you have all the fun!"

Two more police cars arrive, lights flashing. She didn't wish the boy ill, but she wasn't going to harbour any fugitives, either.

"Need to check the other stairwell," she says. "I keep finding it—"

"People leave it open, don't they!" he interrupted, proud as punch.

"Exactly, and that's the last thing we need," she says, brushing past him. His face is contorted with glee, illuminated by the rotating blue police lights.

The studios on this floor are carved up randomly like a badly cut cake. L-shaped, a short dogleg juts parallel to the railway line while the longer part stretches to connect to the section looking out onto the fields. Having only arrived six weeks ago, Connie's still not quite sure how many artists work on this floor. Officially ten, but people are always coming and going, friendly but distant. She suspects they're avoiding her, the newbie who didn't go to art college and chases them for unpaid rent. Uptight and out of place. Tonight, the central corridor is dark; she reaches for the light pull by the door. Nothing. The bulb is dead. She listens. The faint sound of music swells from the end of the corridor. Turpentine and incense mingle in the air. A fire waiting to happen—they all ignore her warnings. She walks along slowly, feeling for the next switch. Here the roof is high and pitched, a canopy of steel trusses criss-cross above her head. Most of this floor has "real artists", or a group of men who'd been to Saint Martins at least. None of them live here, of course. They are professionals. Neither does Alison: her studio is second from the end, the only woman on this floor, her performances derided by the others. Connie knows they are just intimidated; she's heard them talking. She walks down the central corridor towards the sound of an undulating saxophone, its notes growing louder. A sliver of light from under a studio door glows red like an ember. Kieran's.

"Not the first time they've come," Jim calls shrilly after her, his feet tapping on the floor.

The summer before last, someone from the studios had helped a group of travellers patch into the electricity via the second-floor bathroom. They did it for a year before management finally realised.

"Yes, I'm aware of that, Jim."

Kieran's door swings open. "Evening, Connie."

Tobacco and something else. Sugary, feminine. Kieran leans against the doorframe, his shirt unbuttoned. A blast of heat from the gas heater on Connie's face.

"You here about our visitors?"

His long, chestnut-brown hair frames a taut, clean-shaven face with beguiling features. She guesses he is her age, although he acts older, almost weary with experience, as though nothing can faze him. His cool grey eyes fix on hers.

"I don't think you've got to worry," he continues. "Apparently, he's broken a leg."

"How do you know that?" she asks, startled.

"Heard him cry out," Kieran replies, scratching his bare stomach coyly.

Connie holds his gaze for a beat, then turns towards Jim idling towards them.

"Idiots," says Jim, his body deflating at the missed opportunity for mischief.

Connie regains her composure. "I'm checking all the floors, the fire exits…"

Kieran's body blocks the view into his studio. "Poor sod. Different bunch from last time, I reckon."

"You'd know," Jim says.

"What's that supposed to mean?" Kieran replies sharply.

Jim shrinks and scuttles off quickly, waving his bottle dismissively. Connie looks after him, confused, unsure what has just passed between them.

"Anything else I can help you with, Connie?" His lips curl into a slow smile. He likes to say her name a lot.

She ignores his question. "Well, if you hear anything, you know where I am."

He nods but doesn't reply. At the sound of stifled giggles from within the room, he smiles and closes the door quickly. She has never been invited inside his studio. The hook below his name in the spare key box remains empty. She had nagged him at first, it was a fire regulation after all, but he had feigned forgetfulness and she'd given up. She stands in the darkness for a moment hearing nothing. As she walks away, the voices behind the door resume.

Moving down through each floor slowly, along the corridors and out into the courtyard she yawns, a residual tiredness flooding her limbs. She hasn't had a proper night's sleep since she moved in. A constant, niggling feeling in her gut. Anxious, alert to everything. This part of London is still so unknown to her, and this building is an island, surrounded by the fields' dark and empty sea. In the street, the sound of car doors slamming; the police rolling out. The young lad, did they have him? She hopes he's limping down the backstreets: Lamb Lane, or Exmouth Place. Her nan brought her up to respect the police, or fear them at least, but really, she doesn't think anyone has a right to tell other people how to live. Sometimes she worries it's all she spends her time doing. Don't use this gas cannister, do lock up your flammables, keep the corridors clear. One demand after another. What did the artists' contracts say? 'Don't cause a nuisance.' What would she know about it? She's never had the chance to act up, or the right to.

Caretaking isn't even her only job. She also works, for actual money—not much more, but some—as the administrator of 'the Index', an artist registry service in Stepney Green. In her mind, she's already rebelled by leaving Crawley, by escaping secretarial work in a stuffy insurance office, and filing artist biographies in a draughty one instead. It means nothing to this lot. How shocked she'd been to discover most were on the dole. The shame of it. You needed a job. Always. She fishes for the bundle of keys in her pocket and once inside, shuffles towards the living room window, legs heavy, the evening's adrenalin draining out like electricity through an earthed wire. She adjusts the curtains against the glowing streetlight. The lurcher's dark eyes stare back at her, sitting solemnly on the pavement watching the window. She yelps, clasping her hand to her mouth. Forgotten. Poor thing, collateral. The dog stands on its hind legs, pausing for a moment, and then quickly, as though pursued, bolts towards the dark fields.

The next morning

"Just thought I should let you know," Connie says, in the phone box, holding the greasy receiver away from her face.

"Is the building secure?" Fred, the studio manager, replies. His tone is agitated, typewriter keys jabbing in the background. She pictures him in the studio office, cigarette resting in a cut glass ashtray.

"Yeah, yeah, all fine." The phone box stinks of piss.

"Rent's due next week."

"Yup." She hops on the spot, stamping her feet against the cold, trying to avoid the puddle in the corner.

"How are you settling in?"

"Fine."

"Jim behaving?"

"Sure."

"OK, well call me if you need."

Connie replaces the receiver, her coins swallowed by the machine with a loud gulp. Outside, she takes a deep breath of cold air, satisfied that Fred is beginning to trust her. She walks along the empty street back to the studios. To her left, a row of shabby terraces with long slithers of front garden: squats filled with separatist feminists, or the last sorry homes of locals, waiting for the council to move them into something better. Arriving at the corner, she surveys the scene. Skid marks in the road point two giant arrows at the gate. Frozen droplets collect in the steel links of the mangled chain. She crosses her arms and chews the inside of her mouth. She imagines the judder of the gearstick and the vibration of the pedal. The boy had been hurt, Kieran said. She can't see any blood. Maybe he made it; she hopes he did. Some gall. The truck has impressed itself into the gate's surface. It looks dented but resilient, proud it kept them out.

She could do a rubbing—the way people do with trees. By cataloguing the collision, she would make something of it, another kind of material memory. Right now, though, she has work to do.

The front door to the studios is one step up from the pavement. It should be double-locked at all times, but no one ever remembers. Strutting past the cork board, she raps her knuckles along the dated display of yellowing gig posters. She drops the fist of keys into the pocket of her baggy overalls. The thick twill fabric often doubles as a tea towel, or a rag, handprints smeared across her thighs. It made winter in the studio's icy, concrete climate bearable.

She hadn't been able to get back to sleep after her encounter with the dog. Its lonely eyes staying with her until dawn. Over a plate of fried eggs at Pellicci's early that morning, jostled between cabbies and barrow boys, she'd added "Travellers + Electricity?" to the growing list of mysteries recorded in her notepad. As she slurped hot, sweet tea and dribbled yolk across its pages, she reconsidered the other entries: "What has happened to the spare roof key?" and "Who is Thurston Borkis?". "Borkis" was the author of a photocopied circular posted sporadically under studio doors. A suspected pseudonym. Unlike genuine attempts to recover lost items, something which occurred with irritating frequency, these notices sought the useless and broken. Connie had taken it seriously at first, but by the third message—an earnest request for the return of three used tea bags—she'd become suspicious. Someone's idea of a joke? An artwork perhaps? She still can't tell the difference.

Connie picks up the bundle of post from the floor, as the door to the courtyard swings open and a small man wearing a beret holding a rusty saw clatters through.

"Anything for me?" he asks, bobbing on the spot.

"Hang on, let me check—what's your name again?"

He looks offended.

"Er, Mark Kazlauskas."

She flicks clumsily through the stack in the nook of her arm. There are too many names to remember.

She hands over a thick padded envelope with international stamps. He drops the saw to the floor, bending down and ripping the envelope open with both hands, beret flopping from his head. She stoops to catch it. A furrow of scalp visible down the centre of his skull from which two black curtains hang heavy behind jutting ears.

"A-ha!" he cries, springing up with one arm aloft, fist clenched. "Twelve red spools of cotton."

"Is that good?" she asks.

"It is!"

He's like a puppy.

"They're from my Polish contact, Dawid, to add to my red object sculpture."

"Why red?"

"Well, why not?" he smiles, baring both rows of teeth.

"Can't argue with that!" she laughs.

He fumbles to retrieve the saw, nods and turns towards the stairs.

"Remember," he says, "art is fine, food is good. Cheerio!"

Connie sorts the remainder of the artists' post into the kennel of letterboxes. The same people always get post; she isn't one of them. A postcard for Arlo and Des, postmarked Toronto, a banana motif rubber-stamped in red and black ink where a written message should be. Quite the pair. Performance artists and experimental musicians, not from around here. The two of them are always together. Arlo, small like a Victorian street urchin, speaking in riddles, while Des, tall and scathing, is to Connie, the most glamorous woman in the world. They're part of a burgeoning mail-art network, receiving weird salvos from all sorts of places: San

Francisco, Peru, even Sydney. These connections give them an air of superiority. There is also an official-looking letter for Pamela, Private & Confidential printed in the corner. A New York City native, Pamela is almost ten years Connie's senior and her only real friend in the building.

Past the letterboxes, the small courtyard is deserted and cast in shadow: the sunlight is obscured by a metal walkway overhead. It takes Connie ten steps to cross to her flat, with its galley kitchen, bedroom on the ground floor and a work room upstairs. It was the place where the old factory foreman would have lived. Closing the door behind her, the poky rooms appear subdued. She opens the curtains. When she'd first moved in, the downstairs rooms were painted bright red, floor to ceiling. The colour had made her feel as though she were living inside an organ. The previous caretaker, Harold, had lived in the flat with his wife June and their three children. The skirting boards were purple, and upstairs a patchwork of patterned wallpapers—flowers and frills in delicate pink, orange and yellow—covered the rooms. She'd kept slivers of each paint layer and wallpaper sample in a metal pin box like pressed flowers. Sanding had taken days and filled her mouth with metallic-tasting dust. She felt relieved as she rolled the thick white paint in neat, vertical lines. Obliterating their past. Beginning again.

She fills the kettle and places it on the gas hob, then flops down onto the single mattress in her bedroom, its springs squealing under her weight. She pulls the blankets up over her body and dangles her booted feet off the end of the bed. A macramé shawl with dip-dyed fuchsia tassels stretches along the wall to conceal a forked crack in the plaster. A collection of photographs is tacked around the shawl: one showing Connie as a child being pushed on the swings in Crawley, her mum a blur in the background; one of Nan and Pop wedged into a beige sofa, red eyes like shocked rabbits caught in the flash. Family stuff. Things that are supposed to make you feel at home.

Amongst these are the first pictures she took on her Leica: one showing the view from Primrose Hill at sunrise, and the other a dead bumblebee curled on a dusty windowsill. She was proud of that one—she'd really managed to find the light. Her ex-boyfriend Gary had shown her how to use a camera after they'd met at a squat party in Camden, not long after she finished secretarial college. She strokes a straggly tassel. At the time, he'd been a live-in caretaker at the Dairy — a factory round the corner where artists and musicians lived. Lying on a pile of discarded coats, black bombers melting under their tongues, they'd become acquainted; Connie tracing swirls of smoke with an outstretched finger, as he talked about his prog rock band *Goldentoe*.

How much her life had changed since then. No secretarial work, no boyfriend either, thank God. The old Dairy at Prince of Wales Crescent was another era, but it was the beginning of her new life: living in old warehouses and factories, and artists' studios. She'd never slept anywhere as cold as the Dairy before. It was a big, clanking, metallic space. A place for chilled liquids, milk, machines and chemicals, not human bodies. And certainly not warmth. She'd moved in with Gary quickly, desperate to get out of Crawley. The future was waiting. Part of her was glad when *Goldentoe* went on tour, and Gary asked her to take over his caretaker job, her first of that kind. He said, apologetically, "I probably won't be back." Handed her the keys sheepishly. The last she heard, they were the house band at a bierkeller in Dortmund. Sometimes life seemed as fickle as the weather. What if she hadn't been sitting next to Heather at secretarial college, and what if Heather hadn't had an older hip brother, who liked to invite clueless girls to arty squat parties. Where might she be?

Another one of the photos tacked up on the wall is of a Camden Council depot loading bay taken from above. Connie took it during her first months at the Dairy, when she was still familiarising herself with the local area. Council employees had made two mountains of furniture from house clearances: thin mattresses with coiled springs, broken cots, scraps of underlay, bed sheets, whole wardrobes upended. Lives knotted together in precarious formations. Living and working in buildings that were condemned, marked for demolition or refurbishment, created a strange contract between occupant and host. The picture reminds her how intimately involved she was in the entropy of her own habitat, constantly wrestling with nature, with decay, facing the facts of impermanence.

She washes her teacup and places it on the draining board. Time for her walk round. Connie finds these trips a reassuring habit, beating the building's bounds like a medieval villager, working clockwise, moving up and down staircases, undulating through the floors like a wave. For many of the artists, all paths led to their studio and back, the rest remaining a mystery. Buildings only have so many routes; there are the paths getting you in and out quickest, and the paths taken when you don't want to see anyone. Connie walks them all, noting things down in her pad, taking pleasure in noticing the smallest details—yellowing fag butts accumulating in the courtyard drain, or the persistence of a balled-up Sainsbury's till roll on the fourth step of the front staircase.

The first floor is clear. Bill, painter, perpetual coffee breath. Next door to him—Ian, rake thin and sinewy, Australian, recently returned from North America where, as explained to her at length in the pub last week, he'd reached a dead end artistically and emotionally. Jill, one along, does conceptual work—a stocky, self-described "environmentalist", her last sculpture used dry ice and light refracted through glass cubes

45

full of water. These atmospheric interruptions usually seeped into the corridor. Today, it smells of lemon zest and leather.

Connie climbs another flight. Second floor: clear but for one swollen bin bag outside Studio 15. She grabs it with both hands. Sometimes it's just easier to do things yourself. She imagines the spaces behind the walls, seeing through studs, pulling nails from the cladding to expose huddles of men around canvasses. *Is painting dead?* they ask, thumbs tucked in the pockets of maroon corduroy trousers. *Who is art for?* they muse, hunched over stools. Struggling to hold the bag away from her body, she sniggers and heads downstairs to the bins.

The studios are more like a city than a building. In this land of invisible borders there are districts and streets, quarters and turf, and each has its own atmosphere. The basement, reached via the courtyard, is her least favourite place. It's dark and damp; accessible from a set of roughly cast concrete steps that descend at uneven heights to a narrow passageway. Disintegrating walls shed soggy plaster, clinging to Connie's overalls whenever she visits. The exposed passageway is a feeder system for three large subterranean studios; two face the park, whilst the third is a long windowless bunker. First up is Franco, an Italian painter. Quiet and birdlike, his name pasted across his door in letters cut from a newspaper. Next to him, Arlo and Des. She feels so shy and awkward around them, still reeling after their last performance, Arlo strung up on a cross, drenched in a pint of pig's blood, the air stinking of iron. Lastly, in the bunker are Circuit, a group of Ukrainian kineticists, rarely seen in daylight. She worries about the pallid colour of their skin.

Eleven o'clock, all quiet still. Early for this lot. She heaves the bag into the wheelie bin, a burst of turpentine and rotten banana as it hits the decomposing pile. Her stomach churns, and she moves quickly towards the streak of grey sky at the end of the basement passageway. These winter days are too short. Her foot finds the bottom step as the courtyard door whines open just above her. Instinctively, she shrinks back into the shadows.

"Will I see you next weekend?" the voice murmurs, as though cautious.

All Connie can see is their feet. One set: small, female, flat navy-blue T-bars, white socks. The other set: brown boots, male, an inch heel, unevenly worn, the leather creased. She knows these boots; they belong to Kieran.

"Perhaps," he replies.

Connie hears the thunk of the entrance latch.

"But how will I know?" Disappointment.

"I'll find you."

And before she can reply, the boots press forward, the T-bars stumble back and out across the threshold, into the street. All is quiet again. Connie grimaces. How easily some men sought control. The pleasure they took from it. Why? She waits for him to leave. The seconds turn into minutes. What was he doing?

"You can come out now, Connie."

She jumps, as a head of long brown curls flops over the railings. She straightens hurriedly and stumbles up the stairs.

"I was just—" she fumbles for the words, "—putting the rubbish out."

He grins mischievously at her. "Me too."

"What?" she says, frowning. They stare at each other for a moment. His grey eyes soften suddenly, and he smirks, digging his hands into his pockets and pulling out an empty packet of cigarettes. He crushes it in his fist and flicks it over Connie's head. It litters the passageway behind her. He laughs and turns back towards the studios.

"Hilarious," she mutters, as the courtyard door hinge lets out a long mocking squeal. Well, that needs oil. She reaches for her notepad, grappling for the pencil wedged behind her ear, a faint tremor in her hands.

That afternoon

Some artists nest, their spaces evolving into glorified dens of disarray. Others are like science laboratories, sites of experiment and failure. One painter in the basement prepares endless canvasses but, as far as Connie can tell, has never started a painting: rows of blank rectangles line his studio walls, their primed surfaces filmed with dust, waiting. Pamela waits for nothing. She exists in the margins of the traditional workday: printing photographs at dusk and going out hunting for materials before the city wakes. Connie has seen her silhouette moving at the window all hours; she's heard the pad of Pamela's footsteps behind the studio door as she passes during her early morning walk rounds. Her materials are organised in crates and boxes with printed labels, arranged methodically along an imposing industrial shelving unit. Her darkroom equipment is always clean. What she can't find new she sources from trade meets and through classifieds. She cultivates contacts, lenses smuggled from the Soviet Union carefully wrapped in sheets of Cyrillic newsprint.

Contrary to this attentiveness, the studio's concession to domesticity is dysfunctional. Pinched tea bags splatter the enamel sink; a mahogany dressing table leans, ineffective storage for a dented aluminium pot, chipped plates and a few pieces of mismatched cutlery. The dressing table had been their introduction. Connie helped Pamela rescue it from the tip one afternoon in late November. They'd wrestled with it silently across the fields and up three flights of stairs, Connie staring at the back of Pamela's bleached shorn head. On the floor next to the chewed leg of the dressing table is an electric kettle—one of the few on the premises—and a battered double-burner butane stove. No sofa or armchair, only a bed, a slim tatami mat pushed into a corner, hidden behind a bank of tubes storing large rolls of photographic paper.

"I wish you'd get a heater in here," Connie says, cupping her hands to her mouth.

"I don't like the sensation," Pamela replies, leaning her elbow on the brick ledge under the window, the cracked panes taped up, plugged with rags and cardboard.

"What, feeling warm?"

Pamela hasn't left the building in four days. She closes her eyes and rubs the nape of her neck, trying to adjust to having company. Connie sits cross-legged on the floor and fidgets noisily with a bag of strawberry bonbons.

"I don't like those gas things you have here," replies Pamela, her New York City drawl barely hiding its disgust. "They make my head ache—plus, I thought you would appreciate my conscientious approach to fire safety." She gestures to the piles of dry paper, the metal cabinet full of hydroquinone and ammonium thiosulfate.

Pamela scoops up the hot water bottle from her bed and peels off the straggly knitted cover. She'd bought the bottle in Boots her first week in London, having forgotten how cold it was to sleep alone. She fills the kettle and flicks it on.

"You didn't hear anything this morning?" Connie says.

"Ear plugs and a Valium. Forget it."

"Kieran said one of them broke their leg."

"Kieran?" Pamela responds sharply.

"Yeah, he was there, he sort of helped."

"Hmm," she murmurs.

"I saw him earlier today and you're right, he's an absolute lech. Although he was quite friendly yest—"

"I wouldn't trust him," Pamela interjects.

"Don't start with your community politics."

" 'Community' isn't the word I'd choose," Pamela replies. The kettle pings and she fills the pink bottle, squeezing out puffs of rubberised air.

As the studio's caretaker, Connie often feels excluded from its artists' cliques. On a routine walk round last week she'd found proof. A trestle table in the second-floor common area bore the remnants of a boozy fish supper: crushed tins of Double Diamond, encrusted with grey ash; four place settings of translucent newspaper, torn and sticky with tartare sauce. Amongst the debris, a poster had been torn from the notice board and screwed into a tight ball. Instinctively, Connie had smoothed out the paper to reveal a scrawled list of studio residents grouped into tribes. One headed "The Pirates" included self-defined renegades and rebels from posh families: the ones whose teeth were rotten, and voices were plummy. Another, "The Police", had only one name under it: Connie.

"You really want to sit around until three a.m. listening to all that hot air?" Pamela had asked, her voice sharp and impatient. Having the option might be nice.

The studio bursts brightly with clear winter sky and the reaching, leafy branches of a hardened plane tree. Its wooden floor is worn and shiny in patches, marked by years of feet shuffling in front of whirring knitting machines. A large worktable stretches along one wall, above which a grey noticeboard hangs, home to scraps of research material and notes written in haste by Pamela's expressive hands. The other wall is completely clear, a backdrop for photo shoots and sculptural assemblages. Today, there is a new object, a plywood trapezium. This large awkward form reminds Connie of school gymnastics on cold mornings. What makes Pamela special is that despite her meticulous approach, the work isn't precious: it always swells with life. Somehow matter is imbued with spirit, like a stopped heart shocked into beating again. Although she takes photographs, makes performances and installations, her practice can't be defined by medium. She doesn't like labels. Connie often describes her as a sculptor, someone who bends and shapes light, using her body as material as though it were gesso or paper. In this present configuration, the studio is Pamela's stage and Connie, her grateful audience.

Pamela's name was on the list too, also on its own, but written along the edge of the paper, not belonging to any tribe. She spins feverishly in her own micro-orbit. Too preoccupied with her own plans. Always going somewhere, researching something. Having arrived in England six years earlier, Pamela returns to the States every summer, each time threatening to never come back. Determined, obsessive, her knowledge of art encyclopaedic. Her strong face is often stern and unreadable. She gives harsh criticism, but unlike so many of them in the studios, she takes Connie seriously. Connie has tried not to care about The Pirates and The Police, but the malevolent glee of those who'd drawn the overlapping inked circles still hurts.

"Catch!" Pamela says, tossing the swollen hot water bottle. It lands in Connie's lap with a thump.

"It's not studio politics, anyway," she continues, and shrugs. "It's Kieran, I don't trust him." Changing the subject, she says, "Here, take the end of this," and nods at Connie, pulling at the edge of a long, broken piece of Masonite on the unit's top shelf.

The first act is gathering. Pamela trawls the streets nearby, finds patterned threadbare carpets, broken prams and collapsed cardboard boxes. She scours empty building plots for rusty tangles of wire and battered suitcases. Poor condition doesn't matter; it's what attracts her.

"There's a whole pile of boxes outside the butchers on Broadway Market—I saw it on my way to the shop," Connie says, brushing wood chips from her hands and resuming her position on the floor. She looks out for things for Pamela when she's doing her own collections. Connie uses old magazines as well as newspaper cuttings to make her collages, selecting them from "The Waste" on Kingsland Road: a street of market stalls full of girlie mags and second-hand paperbacks.

"I saw that," Pamela says. "Not for me, I decided."

"Yeah, but the ones on the bottom have got bloodstains on them."

"Really?"

"From the meat, I suppose." All the material she has found so far, Pamela hasn't used. She acts unfazed, but each rejection stings.

"What's that?" Connie points at the plywood shape.

"Not sure yet," Pamela replies. "The start of something. I want to see if I can print a photograph on it, capture history in the fibres of the wood."

Connie has started arriving at the studio much earlier than agreed. Pamela doesn't need her for taking the photographs, just printing them. She finds Connie's presence a little invasive, but doesn't have the heart to say so, remembering how difficult things are when you're just starting out. Observation is the secret; how else do you learn to be an artist? And yet it's difficult to get immersed in the process when you're being watched. Giving up, she perches on a high stool and pulls out a flattened packet of tobacco from her back pocket. She nips a brittle tangle into a rizla, rolling it between her long fingers and licking its edge. Connie is hunched up like a gargoyle on the floor beneath her. Pamela tips her head back and exhales to the ceiling joists.

Sometimes she misses the studio she had at the Docks. Tower Bridge was gaudy, the river ancient. It was her first taste of making art over here. She'd felt energised, the ghosts of former use staining the walls and stairwells. The smell of turmeric lingering in the scrubbed wooden floors. It had been a difficult learning curve. Here there *had* been community politics. Shared needs don't always amount to shared beliefs. The memory is bittersweet. Sunny afternoons, legs dangling over the edge of the quay, skimming the oily water of the Thames. The simmering tension amongst artists. The basin, undisturbed by ships, stretched out inert in front of them. She had been in awe of the older artists; she sat on the fringes, listening intently to their heated arguments. One night, Barbara—one of the studio founders, already an established painter—said the use of the term "community" to describe their activities was unfortunate. Unfortunate for you, Pamela thought at the time, because you don't need one. At that moment she decided she was going to be like Barbara.

Seeing Connie now, she feels a pang of guilt for taking advantage of her enthusiasm. Over the last month they'd developed Pamela's photographs together. Her assemblages had got bigger. She'd started working with large format equipment, the entire room being used as a darkroom to get the scale she needed. It's too much for her to do alone now; she needs help moving things around, reading the grain during the enlargement process. Pamela rolls her head from side to side. It's only when she stops that she feels the build-up of the day's work in her muscles.

Working with Pamela like this, Connie feels excited about art; she feels like she can do anything. She watches the bones in Pamela's jaw move as she smokes.

One night, she had said absentmindedly: "There are three of us working in here."

"What do you mean?" Pamela had asked.

"You, me and the building," Connie said quietly, embarrassed.

Pamela smiled. "I'm going to steal that."

Connie had swelled with pride, staying up in her studio late into the night, making collages, immersed in her work.

The stems of wilted carnations crackle in Pamela's hands as she pulls them from a pint glass; a crusted brown rim hovers an inch above the remaining yellow liquid.

"You should throw them out," Connie says. "It's bad luck to keep dead flowers around."

"I was going to use the water to dye something," Pamela says, stubbing out her cigarette in the metal ashtray. She pauses to take a drink of water straight from the tap. She walks back and forth scrutinising the objects assembled in the middle of the floor. Connie finds this protracted choreography captivating. Watching a person caught up in their own mind.

"How's your work going?" Pamela asks abruptly.

"Money-work or artwork?"

"Art of course."

"Erm. Slowly," Connie says. "I've started some new collages. I keep getting distracted by things in the office." Although she's only supposed to work on the Index two days a week, there's never enough time to get everything done and complete all her caretaking duties.

"Maybe it's the same thing? What you do in the office, around the building. It is creative in a way. Systems, structures," Pamela says.

"It could be." Connie sounds unconvinced. "Maybe it is. I'm sort of obsessed with compiling it, to be honest. The Index is hectic, nine new artists a week!"

"Tick boxes, coloured shapes, a kind of diagrammatic poetry."

"The manual monster," Connie says.

"The what?"

"That's what I call it, the Index, it's like a giant Rolodex. One day the metal cabinet that holds all the files will be as big as this room; it's going to be international. The more people are in it, the better it will work."

Pamela narrows her eyes.

"It's the future!" Connie says.

Connie's favourite part of the manual monster is the Index records: pieces of printed black and white card. These records are the key to the Index: they help you access slides of work, copies of any reviews, a CV. Each artist is assigned one when they join. The cards have a complex coded system of categories, from biographical information to basic details concerning their preferred medium. It was Connie's idea to use coloured stickers for each category. She'd thought artists would appreciate this pictorial system. They wouldn't have wanted words describing their work.

"Well, you better make something for the Open Studios," Pamela pushes, determined not to let the matter drop. For the first time, the artists at Tower Street are opening their studios to the public in September.

"I want to," Connie replies, trying to sound confident, her insides churning.

Pamela pulls out a plastic fruit crate full of feathers and strips of animal fur she got down the Goldhawk Road. She listens to Connie intently; this other job makes Pamela think about the slow bureaucracy of her visa applications when she first arrived all those years ago, and about the restrictiveness of architecture. It matters to her how different things interact, layer and align. It's how she works: organic processes and industrial mechanisms in unison. She thinks about the relationship between individuals and public institutional structures, the intimate tensions between strangers. She uses the walls and floor of this building as a frame for her body. Capturing herself among the rotten stuff of the street. Photography doesn't intimidate Pamela. Other women have said the same: it doesn't have the baggage of existing art forms like painting. She likes how it can fix things. A gesture, a feeling. In early experiments, she'd tinted images with chemicals. This reduces the lifespan of the work, but she doesn't care if it doesn't last forever. It seems to Pamela that everyone around her is interested in destruction. Men setting canvases alight, pulling up floorboards and tunnelling underground, exhibiting the ghostly remains of industry. But Pamela, sifting through waste, is interested in reconstitution, what happens after the destruction: which things are conserved, and what is erased.

The short winter day is withdrawing into night. In the studio, the last of the light catches the dust particles in the air. Ribbons of glitter shine through the room and across their faces. They can't start printing until it's completely dark.

"Tea or wine?"

"OK, yeah, please," Pamela replies, stroking a scrap of fox fur.

"Which?"

"Both?"

"Together?"

"Sorry," Pamela says, laughing, "I'm stopping!" She bundles the fur into the box and tucks it onto the top shelf. "I'd like tea to warm me up then a glass of red wine," she says, catching Connie's steadfast eye. She means well. Next door—clomping footsteps; an electric guitar shreds loudly from a tape deck. They laugh.

"I've been thinking about what you were saying before," Pamela starts. Connie holds out the hot mug, gingerly turning the handle towards Pamela. "I don't think they have to be separate. If all the men are making sculptures with steel rivets and bricks, why can't you use typewriter ribbon and paperclips?"

By five o'clock, it's dark enough to print. The red safelight hangs from a hook in the ceiling. At one end of the room is the enlarger, resting on its side, levelled with wooden wedges. The room's entire 16 feet is needed to create the scale of photographs Pamela requires.

"Lights," she says, and Connie flips off the switch.

Pamela slips the first negative in between the bellows of the enlarger. A large rectangle of light hits the wall. "Here you go," Pamela murmurs, passing Connie the grain focusing scope. The small contraption is cold and surprisingly heavy. Connie's shadow interrupts the beam. She places the scope flat against the wall.

Pamela begins to pull the focus. The grains look frizzy like fabric fibres.

"Up a bit," Connie calls.

"How about now?"

"Yes, almost, nearly, a bit more."

Now they look like heads of wheat.

"Too far now, back again slightly."

Sharp worms.

"Lock it."

Pamela has a pulley and rope system rigged in the corner to raise the paper—she needs an extra pair of hands to lift the roll from the sealed lightproof tube and attach it to the pulley. She uses a scalpel to slice the sheet away, leaving the edges jagged. They hold the paper by its corners as they navigate the room, arms outstretched, careful not to touch its surface with their bodies. They tack it up on the wall. Pamela presses the button and light floods the paper for a moment. Seconds later, and the memory of the afternoon is transferred like magic. It doesn't matter how many times they do it. To Connie, it never gets old.

Bones differ in character according to age, the use to which they are put and the existence of disease. In early life they are not fully ossified, whereas in old age they lose their resilience. A much larger quantity of fatty constituents is also present. Where the bones have not been used, they do not possess the same amount of compact tissue and become porous with a much greater chance of fracture occurring.

10 June 2017

We disagreed on curtain colours, compromising in the end with cheap roller blinds. A temporary solution. I stare at the thin plastic dragging along the sill in the breeze until my eyes start to water. Flashes of Croydon Ikea: trolleys manoeuvred across rubber, the walkway a winding conveyor belt of bickering couples.

Another bad sleep: last night's storm breaking the close heat of the previous week, thunder and lightning just before sunrise. Forty minutes of strained expulsions. Never easily disturbed, Jane breathed slow and steady throughout. I watched her face, gerbil-like, nuzzle the pillow. The nights and their sounds don't surprise me anymore. I was scared at first of the pressure, that feeling in my stomach, a deep, deep grief. Now I wait, willing it to come, sensing it most strongly in the early hours while I stare at the steel trusses in the ceiling. The park is hushed as though it senses it too, disturbed only by the beats of an occasional passing car, a muscular heart pumping in a metal ribcage. In the morning light, when the birds start tweeting, the force of the feeling dissipates; it seems foolish. I've stopped telling Jane.

…BBC News. We'll be hearing reports from Venezuela, Ireland, Egypt and India in Foreign Correspondence *in just half an hour. But now, with a discussion about where British politics goes from here,* The Week in Westminster, *presented by Steve Tobys….*

I sit up and hair falls lankly around my face. It's been twelve days since I pulled a soapy knotted tail from the plughole and I haven't washed it since. The joys of working from home. Besides, I like it when I can smell myself: sour, slightly sweet. Downstairs, I hear Jane turn on the tap, water hit the porcelain of our Belfast sink. The block's renovation was already three months behind schedule when they set down the first layers of the mezzanine's composite particleboard floor and insulation. Jane had explained the whole process using the analogy of a trifle. Steel girders formed the structural sponge, yellow mineral-wool quilt spooned like dollops of custard on top. Together these soaked up sound and heat, like a soft cake does sherry. "I've never made a trifle," I said. From downstairs the bedroom doesn't look right. Gone is the clarity of the vaulted ceiling; the mezzanine bedroom swells overhead like a blocked pore.

Hello, and welcome to a special live edition in the aftermath of a historic election...

I kick the bedcovers off and reach for my phone. Two new messages add to the fifty unread. Mum: *Good morning Tamsin, according to the paper early-bird exercisers experience a 50% boost to their feelings of wellbeing. Your father is painting the study again. Off to the tip later. Take care of yourself xx* From smear tests to mole checks or dentist's appointments, nothing gives her more satisfaction than the maintenance of my body. Well, perhaps the surveillance of her own.

I stab the notes app with my finger and type into one headed "Body_Scan": "Fizzy armpits. Hair loss. Toxic paint?" As Mum always says: "cross the t's and dot the i's". I look at my horoscope app: "Take note of who and what makes you feel most at home in your skin. This time is formative." I do a few rounds of Twitter and then Instagram, cycling through each mechanically. I tell myself I need Instagram for work, but mostly I use it to stalk ex-partners and disliked acquaintances, to compare myself with old schoolmates long out of touch. The ones who first called me frigid and then later, slut. My obsessions, Jane calls them all. Disappointingly, my exes' new girlfriends all seem to have private accounts and only first names as handles, making cross-referencing with LinkedIn and Facebook tricky. Using the exes' accounts only then, I search through photos of baby showers, birthdays, renovations, Pride. The comments are somewhat fruitful. What kind of person uses the sunflower emoji?! I switch to "Explore" and scroll through the checkerboard of skin care hacks and pop psychology, hovering briefly over a pink square with the words "Five behaviours safe relationships consistently have" in handwritten script.

Maybe it's time I stopped working from home? I don't think it's good for me. I don't think I can hack it. I open Chrome and search for retoucher jobs in London. I scroll. Freelance. Freelance. Videographer, high-end automotive company. I do like doing metal. Full time though, no thanks. Content Producer for the Institute of Anti-Ageing. Interesting. "The role is a mix of asset creation across photography and motion, as well as editing, cropping and management of these assets for handover to our wider inhouse team." But being on set again? People, lights, tricks. Mirrors, foil, diffusion, reflection. Long days, bad clients. What am I thinking, I can't hack that either.

Footsteps on the wrought iron stairs. I put my phone under the pillow and pretend to be asleep. Jane treads quietly across the carpet and places a mug of tea on the bedside table by my face. She smells of spearmint and pinecones, freshly showered.

"Morning," I say, blinking my eyes open. I'm so good at acting.

"It's all kicking off."

"Really?"

Jane grabs a pair of socks from the chest of drawers and sits at the foot of the bed.

"How long you been awake?" I ask, my toes needling her trouser back pocket.

"Few hours. Thought I should crack on with some things before we start the wall. Remember?"

Oh yes, the wall. I watch her inspect the creases between her toes, rubbing flecks of dirt from the soles of her feet.

"Good idea," I say. I sit up and reach for the mug of tea.

"I'm going to get coffee," she says.

"Oh, sorry. I forgot to get it." I sense her irritation. I wrote a list and everything."

"It's fine," she replies. "Do you want anything?"

"Where are you going?"

"Might try that bakery across the way, pastry chef is a friend of a friend. He rates it."

"Get some bread, will you? Nothing fancy, no spelt or walnut."

"I'll see what they've got."

Next to the doorframe are a dysfunctional family of paint testers. Hasty splodges circling the light switch. It had seemed like the best way to avoid another argument, but now my four shades of white face off with Jane's mustard, plum and sage. Her Eating Room Red and Charlotte's Locks jar with my Cotton, Bleached Cotton, Natural Cotton and Air. Some fundamental disharmony is on display. Of course, her colours are all on trend and therefore already outdated. Jane thinks she's immune to algorithms. I haven't said anything—don't have the heart. How long will these propositions be up for? Even if we could agree, I know we'll pick the wrong one.

Jane stands, pulling the crisp black tee-shirt away from her body. She hates the way it clings. I watch her for as long as I can, her freckled forehead bobbing with each step. She doesn't look back.

With the sun in my eyes, I squint back at our building from the street. Rows of broad rectangular windows in regimented lines; red brick, cracked and crumbled with age and the elements, mottled with a patina of soot. I imagine the workers filing out of the doors, tugging cloth caps over their heads, women pulling wisps of cotton from their hair, laughing, arm in arm. They'd all be dead now. Best case scenario: a bungalow in Shoreham-by-Sea like Nan and Grandad. RIP. They made biscuits down in Bermondsey before moving out. Nan on custard creams; Grandad on bourbons.

The estate agents had laid it on thick about the building's industrial heritage. The developer's brochure full of grainy pictures. "Authenticity sells," Tam had said, rubbing her finger over the cheap print and wondering aloud whether they had added a filter to degrade the images further. Tower Street was a women's stockings factory until the artists moved in. Tam said it was considered a site of cultural importance for avant-garde art, experimental film, industrial music. Although at first, I scoffed, I think about it a lot. I'll never tell anyone this, but I feel like I'm part of the building's story now.

Three-wheeled buggies jostle on the street outside the bakery. The smell of warm dough and ground coffee beans hits me like a smack in the face as I push through the glass door. Clouds of hot air rise and condense as they meet the corrugated metal of the cafe's railway arch ceiling. They're playing "Human Behaviour" by Björk. A train rumbles slowly overhead, masking the hiss of the milk frother and the chatter of two Australian baristas. I'd always loved the smell of bread in supermarkets until I found out it was sprayed from a can to make people buy more. It smelled different after that. I love going into other people's kitchens, unpicking the decisions, observing how they work. It's a tight ship here: an organised counter; consistent colour on the loaves—good shine. I'm tempted by the walnut Rugbrød and a bloated-looking loaf called "The Stockholm", but I play it safe with a wholemeal farmhouse and a small bag of All Press Kenya Mwendi Wega.

"Any drinks?"

The woman at the till has nice dimples. "Just this," I confirm.

"Fifteen pounds thirty."

Jesus. Expensive for the basics. I wince as I take out my wallet. *Must support local businesses.* Besides, this place is different, run by a guy from Clapton, born and bred. I hand over a fifty. Her eyebrows go up at the sight of the note as she fumbles the card reader back onto the counter.

Outside, a crow squawks from a cluster of CCTV cameras overlooking the park. Opposite our flat is an ugly mess of a building. A block of flats with a jigsaw of coloured bricks: red, grey and black with beige pointing. The timber-clad top floor has a roof of slate tiles that slant in opposing directions like a deconstructed Rubix cube. A metal spine of painted blue balconies clings onto one side of the building, each outdoor space a vertebra hosting practically identical scenarios: Ikea lanterns, deck chairs, a collapsible table. Fortunately, we don't have to look at it much; Tam made sure we got a flat overlooking the park. It was more expensive, like a hotel room with a sea view, but her parents had covered the difference. Ever since she told them about the move, they've made their concerns known—about wellbeing, crime rates, Tam's ability to do anything. The kind of concerns that feel like criticisms. They always piss on her parade, a strained bureaucracy of care between them. Fear seems to be their ruling emotion. I've rarely met them in the three years we've been together. Tam keeps them at a distance. I've nothing to say to her mother, and her father gives unsolicited advice on anything from the property market to used cars. I don't even fucking drive. At Christmas, before we moved, Tam had tried to explain her plans for the flat—there were tutorials for literally everything on YouTube, she'd said, underscoring the satisfaction of doing something yourself. I watched as they sucked the enthusiasm out of her. Get the professionals in, her mother kept repeating like a mantra, don't worry about the cost. Tam had lost her temper, her face flushed, "Jane can do anything!" she had spat defiantly. "We will do it together." Her father had raised one eyebrow slowly. I felt embarrassed and said nothing. Just looked down at my trainers.

My job, and the flat… It's a lot to do. But I can do both; I can look after it all. I don't make lists. I have everything in my head and that's how I work. The new shelving unit: the plywood strips are cut and stacked behind the beanbag, although I still haven't cracked how to hold the biscuit jointer. How hard can it be? I've got transferable skills. It's amazing how standing over an eight-ring burner, whacking your pan and working 50 hours a week can dampen all the other stuff. I feel shattered. I need three espressos just to keep my eyes open in the morning. And we've got the food writer from the Guardian coming on Thursday night to review the new menu. That profile for Harpers "35 under 35". So much is happening, and sometimes I feel guilty. Like I'm a part of the problem. But then why shouldn't I get a piece of the pie? If my nan and grandad could see. And here's me doing fucking DIY. Fuck it, I'm ready. First job: the wall. Tam still isn't interested. Doesn't matter, I can bring her round.

The door to the flat closes. Jane's gone. My tongue traces the thick layer of fur covering my front teeth. Hygiene is the first thing to go. I know the signs, when things shift and I slide down into that other place. The place where I'm not well. The bedroom stands rigidly around our things, like awkward teenagers at a school disco, as though embarrassed by the bits of furniture still wrapped in plastic. Why had I forced it? Why did I think this would be different?

Before Jane there was Ally. We met at work, back when I had an office job and thought I might one day be a photographer. Ally had full lips and a bright white smile. At the end of our first day together my face hurt from laughing. I'd rubbed my sore cheeks on the bus home, excited to see her again. We had this connection. She was younger than me, just out of uni, saving money and getting ready to go to America for postgrad. Nine hot months and it was over; she left. I was heartbroken. We tried, but the time difference made the distance feel impossible, as though we were living in parallel worlds. Soon she got a new girlfriend, a jealous one who didn't like the sound of me and my early morning calls. We lost touch. Lately I've been thinking of her again, of our nights together, the way we clicked. Waking in the early hours, her body clammy with sleep, pale puffy nipples studded with beads of sweat and the dark, wet centre of her grey jogging bottoms before I slipped my hand inside. We broke up before we could live together. Probably for the best.

Before Ally there was Toby. The university boyfriend. Without the convenience of an academic calendar our relationship had almost immediately collapsed. At his parents' house that first Christmas I'd failed in my performance of "the girlfriend", Toby reprimanding me gently: I needed to smile, to act more grateful to his parents. I could feel myself withdrawing. Staring blankly at his mother across the table I resolved to dump him. Afterwards, Toby had sat crying on the bed, begging me not to leave and ruin Christmas. The next morning we'd driven back to London in silence. It took me another three years to actually leave.

Toby lived in a dingy ex-council flat in Tufnell Park bought for him by his parents in his third year. I managed to keep my distance at first, rebuffing his requests to move in together and staying instead in a series of lonely sublets. There'd been six months in the box room of a warehouse in Hackney Wick. Toby had affectionately called it "the lift shaft" because that's what it would have been. Silverfish scuttled through the mattress while we slept, curled into each other. One weekend, a sickly rotting smell permeated the flat; my flatmates and I searched everywhere for the source before collapsing, covered in sweat, on the sofa. The following day the Rentokil guy excavated a single dead rat that had "probably crawled in there to die", chewing its way inside the threadbare cushions and into the base. After Hackney Wick, another six months. This time house-sitting for a friend of a friend in Bermondsey, one night coming home to a sink of pantry-moth larvae. Ivory blobs floated dead in the dirty dish water, while hordes of others wriggled, clinging to the ceiling like stars.

And then suddenly the friend of a friend returned, and I was asked to leave. Toby caught me at a weak moment when finding a new place seemed impossible. He asked again, "Why don't you move in with me?" And so I did. I allowed myself to be buried, capitulating more and more to his needs. Walking around Westfield helping him look for work trousers, going on double dates, even holding his hand. Who was that person?

With hindsight, Ally gave me the means to get out. She lodged with an old queer who charged peanuts because they liked the company and offered me her room when she left. Extraction from Toby had been easier than expected; my departure bizarrely cordial. He impulsively sold the Tufnell Park flat. A cash buyer, quick turnaround. I offered to help with the move—it was the least I could do. We spent the final weekend packing up his crummy bloke furniture. Manoeuvring politely around each other. Meanwhile I barely had enough things to fill one box. We pulled the wardrobe out to reveal clusters of dark furred spores along the wall. His mother had gasped and refused to go back inside, spending the remainder of the day locked in the Audi giving little waves and tight smiles to passing neighbours. After Toby and Ally, I'd resolved never to be passive again. To take control. Five years on and I'm learning something else: pursuing the things you want isn't an isolated decision but a chain of events, assertive act after assertive act, and that when what you want changes you can't just click "undo".

From outside, the sounds of middle-aged hipsters. Each weekend, crowds of men dressed like toddlers and clutching biodegradable coffee cups and brown, grease-spotted paper bags of pastry descend on London Fields. Striped knitted jumpers, "quirky" socks, expensive brogues, yellow rubberised raincoats with big round buttons and little woolly hats rolled up on the top of their balding heads.

Last Sunday morning we woke up to breaking news of the attacks at London Bridge. Now it's the election. How quickly London forgets. That part of the city always makes me think of Ally. We used to go to Boro Bistro after work, a silly place full of bankers with big bums and shiny broken noses. I remember the first attacks too, ten years before that, the first summer at university, walking back home from work. None of the underground was running; people were everywhere. I went to meet Toby at Liverpool Street. "Fuck!

It's like a festival," he'd said, and I'd grimaced but agreed, because it was. When the bombs went off that morning, I'd been on the Tube but in a different tunnel, on the Hammersmith and City line. The looks on people's faces as they listened to the announcement... Panicked half-runs in pencil skirts. The sudden awareness of being deep underground. Everyone walking as a crowd over London Bridge, marching to our prospective desks. Right past Boro Bistro, not knowing what would happen there ten years later. At the time, Toby had a summer job working for a council-backed energy commission, sorted out by a friend of his father's. In lieu of an actual job this had been deemed "character building". Toby spent his days walking around Barking knocking on doors persuading people to consider discounted re-insulation packages. He had stories of people with no furniture in the house because they had burnt it all for warmth. "Dickensian!" he'd said, shaking his head, over pints in the Drunken Monkey, the smell of the city—carbon monoxide, cooking oil and tobacco—lingering on his shirt.

Work gets into your body. Jane always says this, recalling a hairdresser friend who found an ingrown hair in the pink areola of her nipple. Retrieving it with tweezers, she realised the coarse black hair belonged to one of her clients. Clipped with blades it had found her breast and taken root.

Once, during a long and unsolicited explain-o-thon, Toby said that animals like sheep and cows were described as ruminants, meaning they regurgitate their food and chew it over and over again. This image comforts me on days like today, as if the memories I constantly replay could be a form of nourishment.

The bedroom floor is littered with crumpled clothes removed mechanically from our bodies over the course of the week. On Sundays Jane returns these to the wardrobe or laundry basket, demonstrating her annoyance at my lack of co-operation with quiet sighs and stony looks. A windfall of black socks, squirreled off Jane's toes, lies at the base of the bed. I pick one up and dust motes fall onto the bedsheets. The stiff folds smell strongly of old sweat, Jane's skin and the plastic of her work crocs. I stuff it in my mouth and scream.

There are some diseases where structural damage to the body's soft tissue re-grows as bone. Tendons, ligaments and muscle heal into a secondary skeleton. As with all things, this accrues over time. It can take forty years for disease to put a stop to suppleness, halt all movement. Forty years until total ossification.

21 March 1975, six months before the Night

The girl has always wanted to break a bone. Desperately. Her brothers Terry and Sid had broken an ankle, an arm and three fingers between them from football and scrapping. It wasn't that she coveted their boyhood or unruliness; the point was they'd come to school with limbs strapped up and dunked in plaster. Everyone gathering around in the schoolyard wanting to sign their names. Night after night she'd thrown herself from the bed, crushing her shoulder into the carpet. Her mum banging on the ceiling with a broom handle, practically waking the whole bloody street! She didn't want to break anything serious: a wrist bone would be just fine. She wanted people to gather around, to poke and press her. She wanted to feel her body heal.

She sits on his bed and waits for him to come back. The bruises make her feel grown up. She admires the patterns on her bare legs, each one different: a florid purple tidemark, rusty looking ink blots, a neat row of sallow crescent moons. She knocks her bony knees together. He said these marks were a reminder of how much he loved her. Wanted her. These reminders appear on her skin days later, delayed like love letters sent in the post. They showed she was his.

He cooed to her, "Come on baby, aren't you sweet," and, "That's right, baby." The pride she'd felt at being good. At seeing his eyes roll back. A grown man go all floppy just like that. She hadn't meant to lie. He hadn't asked if she'd done it before, so she hadn't told him. Afterwards he'd said blood was normal; he'd said he liked it. It was only as he got up to light a cigarette, tight curls of hair swirling across the backs of his thighs, that she realised he wasn't so tall. She always thought she'd be with a tall man. It's his boots. Sally at school said anyone can wear heels, even boys.

He's nothing like any boy she's met before. When he uses those long words, the ones she doesn't know, he looks down at her over the bridge of his nose. She wants to giggle at his serious gaze, but she doesn't let on because he doesn't like it when she laughs. He can be horrible. Those curling eyelashes, the way he looks at her, how her stomach flips.

She watches the last smoking stalk of incense droop and fall into a mound of ash on a ceramic saucer. He was just popping out, he said, and wouldn't be long. She is locked in like usual. He didn't like people here knowing his business, he said, and she wondered if that was true or if he in fact didn't trust her. The first few nights she had been in there with him, she'd gone home and run into the bathroom quick. Washed her clothes in the bath for fear of stinking. She couldn't keep that up. Now she hides her school clothes behind the bins in the back garden. She changes in the darkness amongst the slugs and rhododendrons before she goes inside.

How can she convince him she can be trusted? Can she be trusted? She wonders this herself sometimes. She's getting bored now. Won't be a sec, he said. She sits up, pulling a dark-green wool blanket around her bare shoulders, its coarse fibres scratching her skin. The mattress lies on the floor, pushed into the far corner of the room. Such a big place for one man. Huge, twice as big as her mum's front room but twice as empty. Not a stick of furniture. Well, except for the chair he gets her to sit on for his photographs. As far as she can tell, the heater and the metal cabinet were there already. They had other people's names written on them. One wall is covered in pictures and news clippings, all sorts of things, and another is completely clean—bright white clean. In front of it, his easel.

He doesn't like her touching his work. He likes talking about it and he likes her to listen. All this being seen and not heard has taken some getting used to. Staying silent has taught her things: how to move, what he likes, maybe even how to think. One day she'll go to all the far-flung cities he talks about and send him a postcard from every one.

Usually, the cabinet is closed. Today, the door is slightly ajar. She fidgets, craning to see inside from her position on the bed. She's a right nosey parker, her mum says. But curiosity has also been her gift. How else will she learn? Curiosity is what will get her out of this stinking corner of the world. She gathers the blanket around her and tiptoes across the room.

She pauses in front of the cabinet straining to hear the sounds in the corridor outside. He'd hate it if he knew she was looking through his things. A feeling of quiet trepidation settles within her. Pushed to the back on the top shelf is a metal box. It's smaller and leaner than a shoebox, with spring lock catches. There are stencilled numbers and other markings on the side. It looks like a secret. She licks her lips. The box is cold and heavy in her hands, so much heavier than it looks! He would be angry at her. Her heart races. She unclips the lid.

Inside are photographs of girls. Girls like her. She twists her head, contemplating their angles. All naked. Wrapped in cloth, their bodies perching on *her* chair. Some are coy and some are not. Scared. Gangly, arms and legs still too long for them. Small dark nipples and bony hips. The photographs are black and white, their skins are all different shades. They have props: bricks between their thighs or cushions over their faces or logs beneath the arches of their feet. Eyes stare back at her. Some look in pain, twisted into configurations she knows herself. No need to imagine. She pictures him behind the camera. Pressing the shutter. Each girl waiting for his particular signal, an expression flickering in an instant across his face. The same signal he gave her that first day. She knows its power. She feels a stab of jealousy. Her mouth dry, she puts the girls carefully back inside the box and clips the lid down firmly. She nudges it back into place on the cabinet's top shelf, her legs shaking as she teeters on tiptoes. He will be back any minute. She lies down on the mattress and waits, trying to rationalise her discovery.

Perhaps it's not a surprise? Maybe he's been perfecting his craft on them, getting it just right for her. Play is necessary, that's what he says. She can't rob him of this: his process, his gift. Every performance has a dress rehearsal and now he's ready for her. Every artist has to have someone to practice with, don't they? Anyway, as far as she sees it, this is a mutual arrangement. Isn't she using him too? To learn about sex, how to handle herself, culture, politics, radical ideas? How else would she make it out there? Soon she'll have honed these skills; she's going to travel the world.

Three months later

Shielded by his potted plants, Jim stares at Connie. They've flourished these last five years; a lush canopy has unfurled across the studio's steel-framed windows. Through the fronds of a Dypsis lutescens he watches her remove the wallpaper in the flat's upstairs room. Tentative at first and then decisive, reaching, fingers scrabbling at the dank wall's crumbling plaster surface. Piles of torn paper form around her ankles. He presses at the soil of his pots with ink-stained fingers. Rivets have formed in the dry brown earth, contracting with lack of moisture. The larger Monstera deliciosa droops, its robust stem craning over his head to dangle unsteadily above the greased spindle of the printing press. He doesn't like flowers, too feminine, prefers grasses and, when the wet and cold English weather allows it, the succulents of his Turkish homeland. Not that he has seen it for many years nor claimed this heritage, having visited only twice in his lifetime. Both times as a young boy, when his *dede* died, and a year later when his father did. Shortly after this, his given name, Yakup, had been anglicised to James and then shortened to Jim. It is better, he has learned, to keep such discrepancies a secret. The English are an ignorant sort and, in these parts of the city, violent. He learned early how to keep himself safe. Tower Street, his creative fortress, keeps him safe.

She appears to have lost interest in the wallpaper and is attempting to remove the metal grate shielding the bottom portion of the window. Jim feels his jaw clench with irritation. She can never just let things be. Always meddling. Harold had installed them across his windows within weeks of arriving. Some people might have thought him paranoid, but Jim reasons that it's good sense to protect one's family, to want privacy. She looks up at the newly exposed glazing and he ducks behind a palm. She can't see him. He's sure. This is the game, the fun of living like this. When he re-emerges, she's rolling her overalls down to her waist. It's heavy work for the summer; she must be sweating. Irritation gives way to a ringing in his ears as she reveals the flushed pink of her toned arms. She rubs the back of her hand across her forehead, and then across her thigh. He clears his throat and looks away, feeling self-conscious. Perhaps she's regretting it, the task at hand. Jobs always take longer than anticipated.

He does not like change. Change is disruptive. For some time now, he has been attempting to confront his fear of change, which really, is a fear of death, he supposes. Change is temporal, it marks the shifting of time. All things rot. As a keen gardener, he understands the cycle of life. That things grow from seed, bud, bloom and then break down, become mulch. The mulch is as important as the seed. And yet he can't bear to watch petals fade and wrinkle. No, he does not like change. The predictable rhythms of Tower Street have kept him safe these last few years. Calm. But she, he feels instinctively, threatens that.

A sharp intake of breath, a slow exhalation. The air is close, the midday sun slowly transforming the studio into a greenhouse. There is a meeting later for all the artists in the building and Connie will need to be there to take the minutes. She'll be out of his way in just a few more hours, he can walk the building like he used to. Bliss.

Bracing herself with a steady stance, Connie grips the smooth handle of a slotted screwdriver. It's no use. Her hands are too slippy and the screw doesn't budge. From beyond the tight lattice of the window grate streams the full light of the day, with its promise of bright working conditions. She beats the grate with a clenched fist and it rattles defiantly in response. What the hell had Harold been so scared of? She sits on the floor, deflated and hot. A stupid idea to do this on a day like today. Scraps of darkly coloured wallpaper scatter across the floor's narrow boards; a pile of pulverised debris accumulates in one shaded corner. Now two hours in, the room has truly shed its skin. It might not look like it, but she is making progress. It feels as though dust has entered every follicle and crease in her body. Particles hang in the air as rays of sunshine project an elongated image of the window frame onto one wall's mottled surface. Connie is mesmerised by the melding of geometry and memories. Underneath the darker wallpaper are seams of paler base layers which creep towards the window like plants craning for light.

This is the kind of work that gets worse before it gets better. There's a goal here, a focus: she needs a dedicated space to work. She isn't satisfied carving out a corner in someone else's studio anymore. No slice of a man's dark room. Women have been sneaking into men's spaces for long enough; it is time she claimed her own. Roused, she stands and unbuttons her overalls, rolling the thick twill down to her hips and tying the arms together in a knot at her waist. Taking the screwdriver in hand, she sets her jaw as the metal grooves make contact again. On the second attempt, just as she feels the handle begin to slide, the screw turns.

Dust is a fascinating material. It's predominantly dead skin, and the by-products of other matter. A combination of materials, then, lacking essence in and of itself. Jim tries to think about what first attracted him to dust. Hippy psychobabblers might say it was on account of his alienation from his ancestors, those who had lived and died in arid lands. Irrelevant. He prefers to see his interest as stemming from his antagonistic relationship to work. Dust is an irritation: unsightly, a potential harbourer of disease, something in the way. To make an artwork out of dust is to be useful then. And cheap. Very cheap. He likes that especially. Economic in other ways too. From now on he will never waste material. There's nothing to waste because his material *is* waste, the stuff no one wants.

At first, he was reticent to call his dust project an artwork. Initially he thought he was just cleaning up, sweeping the corridors as a form of meditation. Then he remembered an article he'd read about recent developments in so called "earthworks". Artists building sand sculptures on beaches or treating grass like a canvas—walking back and forth making marks with their feet. Being a printer, someone bound to the space of the page, he's never identified with this approach. He's in unchartered territory, but there's no denying a shared sensibility. The site for the project had revealed itself by accident six months ago. Jim likes to take his coffee each morning on the building's flat roof, standing to survey Hackney's soot-covered buildings, as he waits for the sediment to settle in his small glass cup. He'd always assumed the section jutting upwards, obscuring his view of Broadway Market was the additional height needed for the goods lift to clear the top floor, but that day, who knows why, something troubled him. He was willed to investigate. Approaching the rectangular protrusion, a line of hinges appeared. As clouds of hot breath smothered his tingling hands, he prized open the hatch to reveal a collection of old tools smeared with grease, bits of lift cables, a box of matches. Stuck to one side of the cupboard were yellowing magazine clippings of reclining buxom women, a date on one crinkled corner read July 1951, the publication name, *MEN ONLY*, printed in threatening black letters alongside it. What to do with this tomb, this industrial coffin?

He sensed the importance of its discovery. It felt almost spiritual. A place in the building no other eyes had seen nor hands disturbed for a very, very long time. A week passed and he did nothing. Then, bang, an idea. He would fill the cavity with his dust. Preserve these objects of Britain's industrial past in the skins of its descendants. He understands the sweeping of the stairwells as preparation for this task. It is as though he has always been meant to make it. The whole process unspooled in his mind without a snag or tangle. First, a slow accrual of matter in the corners of each stair, all the bits falling off the body during movement. Seven days of compilation before collection. Then transference: the material filed into the roof cupboard like a wad of receipts. His version of an earthwork.

Jim fills an old jam jar with water and pictures the cupboard. Is it strange how much he thinks about it? This project, although artistic, functions to him as a valve of sorts. A letting go of something. Just because a clear reason for doing it has not yet presented itself does not mean it is unworthy of doing. His English aunt, a god-fearing woman, showed him this, the importance of creating rituals to cope with the world. An earthwork, according to the Americans, is a direct intervention into the land. But London is not California, and instead of black basalt rocks or great salt lakes, he makes do with polyester fibres and industrial emollients.

Now the dust cupboard is nearing capacity. Wrenches and coils of old rope are hidden under layers of fine silt collected from the building's corridors. Things are getting delicate. He needs to be careful when opening the hatch, to ensure the wind doesn't undo his work. He wonders whether the hatch is really a manifestation of his mind. With time he fears it has also become delicate, contained but barely containable.

Jim watches the tepid water pooling momentarily on the surface of each plant's parched soil. Tenderly, he shakes the terracotta pots and the liquid disappears. Once the cupboard is filled, Jim supposes the artwork will be finished. Should he show it to anyone? Does it need an audience? He chuckles at the thought of hosting a private view up there, and then another thought hits him and he frowns: no one would come, not for him. He sets the jar down and looks again at Connie's window. Where an ashy metal grill once concealed, now a translucent screen of glass shone. There, in all its crumbling glory, is the upstairs room of the caretaker's flat. Clear as day. Connie, however, is nowhere to be seen. His stomach flips with excitement. The meeting has started, time to begin.

The meeting had been in a sweltering top-floor studio, and Connie is now relieved to be back in the relative coolness of her flat. She squints to decipher the sentence twisting vertically up a page of her notepad. It's difficult to write minutes when people speak so fast. She had to get it all down, and yet, how could she? The woman who writes minutes—and it is always a woman—can only ever be a scribe, a translator of action. All the while holding her tongue, trying not to interrupt the shirtless, gesticulating men. At least, finally, the artists had reached an agreement. The Open Studios would go ahead slightly later than planned. Management had been resisting on account of health and safety. A fire risk. The general public in the studios—it hadn't been done. What about insurance, and how would the artists keep things safe?

Connie looks at how the room is progressing with fresh eyes. Not a bad effort. Harold's chest of drawers and moth-eaten curtains still need getting rid of. She's fed up with the stuff, all these traces of him. The minutes can wait. No one reads them anyway. Throwing the notepad to the floor, she reaches for a broom and begins to sweep up the remaining fragments of wallpaper. She too has thoughts about fire, almost fantasies. How easily she can picture a smouldering cigarette dangling from a sleepy hand. Can feel it falling among wood chips, smell the rags soaked in white spirit. The flames licking quickly, the flickering crackle of paper engulfed, rayon melting into a molten rain, ceiling a rolling canopy of black smoke.

Fire destroys more than people. The management's anxiety was about lost assets as much as lost lives. The solution: additional walk rounds and a visitor register. With these measures in place, the studios can be opened up. The people will be allowed in, and why not? Connie, still so insecure about her knowledge of art, feels more in touch with this mysterious public than the artists she's surrounded by. Despite Pamela's encouragement, she still doesn't know if the things she creates can be called art, and yet, she wants to keep making. What better way to spend her days? Definitely not getting married. She had watched her mum disappear, lose the edges of herself. No children either please, thank you. She might not be able to have a career like the men, but she'll always find something to do.

Removing the window grill has revealed Jim's proximity. Despite her feeling of unease, she finds his window of leaves reassuring. At least he cares for something. She runs her palm across the chest of drawers. Its yellow pine is smeared with the sticky handprints of Harold's children, the wooden surface marked with felt-tip pens. She traces grooves and indentations: jagged hearts and star shapes carved with some sharp implement. She wraps her arms around the drawers to test their weight. As the bulky frame moves from its position against the wall, shifting slightly under her grip, there's a soft crash, a flutter of pages, as something falls to the floor. Crouching down, she reaches under the drawers, her outstretched fingers brushing the edge of an object. Pulling it free, she stands and contemplates her discovery. An exercise book, dog-eared, pages curling, "Rosemary" written in the top corner in a slow, meticulous hand. The book is full of drawings. In one: a family at the beach, dense areas of yellow and blue crayon turning the pages waxy; a man with wild hair; a woman and three children of different sizes; mermaids and leaping fish. In another: dinosaurs with long necks and green scales lope over purple hills. Towards the end the drawings change, becoming sparser and more fragmented, as though their executor lost interest. One page is filled with the same drawing of boots. Brown boots with wedge heels, brown boots with laces. The last is a picture of a person, a man or woman—it's not clear. Whoever it is has been wiped from existence, their face obliterated by the angry scribbles of a black pencil.

One month later

Pamela, fresh from her latest American odyssey, looks lean and vulpine sitting at the table in Connie's bedroom. She nudges the soggy remains of a quiche Lorraine around her plate and recalls her month on the road. Connie listens intently, hanging on her words. Pamela had driven from New York up the East coast in a rented car: Poughkeepsie and the Catskills, Saratoga Springs.

"Manchester! In America?" Connie says.

Pamela laughs. She had carried on going north; she loved the beautiful barren coast. Through Vermont and then Maine, crossing the Canadian border, hitchhiking when her money ran out. She had spent the last week in a cabin on Prince Edward Island. After so much time on her own she's still adjusting to conversation.

"So, what did I miss?" Pamela says as she leans into the stiff back of Connie's salvaged wooden chair. She takes a drag on her cigarette and sets it burning in the ashtray.

"Not much," Connie replies. "A few openings. It's been busy. Hardly saw anyone. Open Studio planning mostly. It's September, you ready? I'm excited." Connie fidgets, while Pamela nods slowly and blows a jet of smoke from her pursed lips.

"What you going to show?" she asks Connie, flicking ash onto the plate.

"I'm getting into a rhythm. Started on a new collage last week. I've more space upstairs now. What about you?"

"I'm thinking of getting a photocopier. It's big in the US. No faffing around with dark rooms. Instant pictures."

"That's cool."

Pamela always had something new. Connie changes the subject, eager to stop jealousy creeping into her thoughts. "I wanted to show you something," she says. She grabs the exercise book from the floor by her bed and hands it to Pamela. "I found this wedged behind that old dresser upstairs. I think it must have belonged to one of the kids. It was sort of hidden. Hidden or forgotten I don't know."

"What do you mean?" Pamela asks, bemused. She opens the book slowly and turns the crumpled pages.

"Creepy, isn't it? But then maybe children's drawings always are. Did Harold and his family mix much with other artists?" Connie can hear how quickly she's talking and pauses to take a breath. Pamela stops at the page with the person and their disfigured face. Connie swallows.

Pamela still hasn't replied to Connie's question, her finger slowly tracing the swirling indentation of the crayon on the paper.

"Those boots," Connie says, "they look familiar to you?"

Pamela's finger stops moving.

Connie pushes her plate to the side and reaches for her wine glass. "Kieran has a pair of boots like that."

"I'd stay away from Kieran if I were you." A flicker of tension in Pamela's jaw.

"Why? You always say you don't trust him, but you never explain," Connie says. She's started, so she commits. "Tell me. I need to know."

"Do you really want me to go into it?"

"Yes!" Connie replies.

Pamela sighs. "Look, it's ancient history. It doesn't matter anymore."

"It matters to me. I need to know what I'm dealing with."

Pamela lets smoke curl out of her mouth slowly. "We met one night in a pub in the West End. It was after an opening at the ICA."

Connie sits up. "When was this?"

85

"Years ago. Just after I moved into the studios at the Docks. The show was in October '68. He just materialised one day. We got on immediately. He talked about finding death in photography." She laughs. "I suppose his darkness suited my mood at the time. I was having trouble producing anything I cared about. I wasn't working."

"I can't imagine you not working," Connie says.

"He had these intense eyes. He cornered me, I told him about the Docks and then somehow, before I knew it, he was there. He got in with Barbara. I don't really know. I wasn't paying attention; I had my own problems."

"Did he say he was an artist?"

"Well, yes, it seemed so. But I never saw anything he made to begin with. He was around all the time. He asked a lot of questions, which, you know, is strange for a man. For them to ask you about yourself. He was interested."

"What did you talk about?"

"My despair over painting—I'd had enough of it by then. It felt meaningless, bourgeois. I was working on these striped canvasses, contrasting colours, optical effects." She took another long drag on her cigarette. "I guess that was quite strange. During all these conversations he never told me he painted. The first thing I knew about it was when I walked into his studio there—there were stacks and stacks of them."

"What kind of paintings?" Connie asks.

Pamela fidgets in her seat. "Well, they were abstract, geometric, repetitive, stripes. Contrasting colours."

"Optical effects," Connie finishes.

"I know," Pamela laughs. "I sound ridiculous. Everyone was doing this stuff back then. But it was just that we had sat up talking late into the night, for weeks, going deep. And when I think about it now, I learnt nothing about him. Not even that the whole time we were talking he was making the same kind of work."

"Jesus, what an arsehole."

"No, but you see, he wasn't nasty—he just pretended like we hadn't had this connection, like I was stupid for finding it strange. I couldn't even say anything. I felt robbed." She smiles ruefully, her lips stained with wine.

"There's something else. I'm still confused about it. I don't even know what I saw exactly; I don't think I saw anything." Pamela stubs out her cigarette.

"What do you mean?"

"No one would have believed me. It was a split second."

"What was?"

She pulls her fingers roughly over her scalp.

"We were inside an inflatable artwork at the Docks."

Connie nods.

"They were all the rage then—a lot of men making them—these huge phallic zeppelins that you could go inside."

"Yeah, yeah, I know the ones you mean," Connie says.

"Well, I remember it was hot. I was wearing a grey tee-shirt and I had these great big rings of sweat under my armpits. The plastic of the inflatable was like a greenhouse magnifying the sun's rays. They had been working on this one floating out in the river basin for ages. It was moored to the Docks while Greg, the artist, experimented with the air pressure, making sure the seams sealed properly. It was a giant plastic tapeworm bobbing on the black water like something from the future." Pamela uncrosses and re-crosses her legs. "He liked to pile people in and film it."

"Sounds fun." Connie says, her eyes wide.

"Well, as you can imagine, it was always a bit of a riot—the plastic bobbing under your feet, bodies everywhere. You couldn't balance, not with the water like it was. There was a lot of trust involved. They were really quite dangerous. The plastic was heavy. I mean *really* heavy. Imagine if it collapsed on you? Death by vacuum pack." She shudders, sparking the lighter.

"It was sexy, too, of course," she says, smiling, and a stream of smoke mushrooms from her lips, "because you could touch each other. Well, you *had* to, you fell into each other by accident, but also, you wanted it for reassurance. It could be liberating, arms and legs colliding, hands everywhere. Some people used it as an excuse to feel you up. The further away from land you ventured, the further the whole thing sank into the water."

Connie nods and rolls her eyes. Part of her wishes she'd had the nerve to try out the one at Hackney Marshes festival last summer.

"Anyway, there must have been ten of us in there. I was at the back of the group, taking it steady, and Kieran was in front of me. We hadn't really spoken since, you know, but I was aware of him that day, checking where I was, that I hadn't snuck off. We caught each other's eye and he grinned, so I grinned back inanely, reacting more than anything. He still felt like a stranger to me. Suddenly he drops to his knees like *whoosh*, down, and I think, oh I get it, he's going to try and drag me down with him. I can see him now, clear as day. The texture of his shirt, the hair around his face. Eventually, I was curious, so I catch up to him. I touch his shoulder, he looks up, and then I see it: this glint of metal, this light in his hands, cupped, resting on his jeans. A pen knife, like the kind Boy Scouts have: red handle, short blade. It's shining, aimed at the plastic floor beneath our feet."

"Wait, what?"

"I don't know. I still don't know. He just kept looking up at me and laughing and then back down at the plastic. I've got goosebumps just thinking about it."

"What did you do?"

"I froze. I couldn't say anything, my mouth just sort of opened and closed like I was a fish."

"What did he do?"

"He just kept smiling. The blade poised. It felt like forever. I imagined it all: the structure collapsing, feet plunging into water, plastic pressing down on our heads."

"Oh God," Connie says softly.

"I imagined the whole thing and he saw it on my face. He just laughed. I looked again at his hands. The blade was gone, and he was on his feet grabbing my hand and dragging me after the others." The cigarette sizzles as she stubs it out on the plate.

"Do you think he actually wanted to do it?"

"I think he wanted me to know he *could* do it."

"Did you tell anyone?"

"Tell them what? Nothing happened."

Connie doesn't reply.

"Why would people listen to me, anyway? He was so popular, and so charming. He still is. I stay away from him now. I don't know who he is. Can't trust him. I stay away, and I suggest you do too."

"Why didn't you tell me before?"

"Plenty of people do strange things. I don't like gossip. I don't like thinking about all the things I failed at during that time. It's not me anymore. I tried to tell my ex, but he thought I was making it up, or, well, reading too much into it—being hysterical."

"I don't," Connie says.

"It's easier here—better managed, and we're creating our own spaces. At the Docks it was a free for all."

Connie feels a momentary surge of pride for the building.

"I know I sound like a broken record, but my advice: stay away from him."

"I just don't like not knowing things," Connie replies, her mind racing.

"Oof," Pamela exhales. She notices her empty wineglass. "Can we talk about something else now?" she asks.

Two weeks later

Connie unchains her bicycle from the gates outside the office and hops on under the threat of a darkening sky. The summer air is dense and sticky. She stamps hard on the pedals as she rides, fighting to beat the storm before it breaks. Her forearms flex, gripping the handles in determination. Straight down the Mile End Road, turning right at the junction, past the Blind Beggar leering at the corner. The drinkers inside appear moody through the dirty glass panes. The East End still looks like the war just ended, forgotten, while the rest of the city moves on. Earlier that summer the National Front had come along this stretch of road, as though they too marched out of another time. She shouldn't have been shocked, not considering the name the newsagent called her black cat. Still, it had frightened her, the huddles of pudgy white men with hate-filled faces. She swerves to avoid kids playing football in the street, the white outline of goalposts daubed on bricks. She pelts recklessly past the mechanics, the bombed-out houses and empty plots, crumbling piles of rubble overgrown with the towering purple stalks of rosebay willowherb. She loves cycling around London—on a bike, you are free.

At the junction of Roman Road, the street sweepers are cleaning up after the market. Calls and whistles of relief at the end of a working day. Misspelt graffiti— BAYCITYROLLERS— is painted in six-foot letters under the bridge. The canal. The greengrocer's awning, a blur of green stripes. There are chatty, hairnet-wearing women inside. People who are polite but suspicious of her, especially when she once asked for garlic. Blank expressions. "You what, love?"

The local newspaper had begun to write articles about the delayed development of Broadway Market, encouraging claimants to know their rights. Perhaps things were changing, slowly. It was hard to imagine the future coming here any time soon. She turns off Mare Street just as the rain begins to speckle the warm pavement, her tyres bouncing over potholes under the railway arches as the studio comes into view. Three kids playing on the corner scatter, squealing as thunder cracks. Connie props her bike against the wall, and fumbles for her keys. She sees a red-haired girl trying to shelter under a big tree with broad leaves on the edge of the park. *Unlucky.*

The summer has dragged on and she almost welcomes the rain. At first, she'd been excited to feel the building's temperament change. Places sealed off during the winter had been blown open as the days grew longer and warmer. Holes unstuffed, doors propped ajar, blinds pulled low to prevent the bleaching of paper or drying out of clay. The swirling summer breeze dislodged dust from windowsills lined with jam jars of mismatched screws, turpentine dregs and dead flies. It swept through open doors, coiling around the grease-coated threads of machinery, carrying the fumes of mineral spirits down to the courtyard where they mingled with the scent of a rosemary bush she had planted in a bucket.

Like a big, lumbering animal coming out of hibernation, the building's heart rate had risen gradually. Its top floor, with skylit pitched roof, became hot like a greenhouse, while the basement kept the atmosphere cool like a fridge. Everywhere there were porous membranes: music was heard through the plasterboard, sweet hash smoke mingled with food turning putrid. Flies thumped at the windows; ants were coaxed into puddles of spilt beer and tabby cats splayed their white bellies basking in the sun. With Pamela away, Connie, like the cats, has spent most of her summer evenings alone, lounging in a sagging deckchair on

91

the roof drinking gin sodas, while absentmindedly reading, the bitumen soft and sticky underfoot.

Opposite the studios, the All Nations club waits expectantly for tonight's punters. Every Saturday it plays reggae and soul until the early hours. Connie likes watching the couples' step from their gleaming Cortinas or Cavaliers, shattering the dreary streets of Hackney with bright silk dresses and flared suits.

She swings the entrance gate open and wheels her bike inside. The caretaker's flat still smells of this morning's burnt toast. She grabs a bottle of milk from the fridge and throws her bag through the beaded curtain screening her bedroom from the rest of the flat. She leaps up the narrow staircase two at a time and arrives at the upstairs studio out of breath. The room is in disarray after a frantic late-night session. A cork board on the wall above her desk is covered with newspaper and magazine clippings. Below it, empty glue pots, blunt scalpel blades and pieces of coloured card lie discarded. Slivers of paper scatter the bare floorboards around her chair like confetti.

Pushed to one corner of the desk is a typewriter and the documents for the forthcoming Open Studios event. Connie is in charge of compiling material for the catalogue in a manner not dissimilar to the Index. She still needs to chase up artists who haven't provided statements, photographs and biographies. The artists she thought would give her the most problems, Arlo and Des, have surprised her. Despite their anarchic presentation and their subversive tendencies, they promptly delivered a stack of neatly typed pages: an extensive account of exhibition dates and other details. It is the other, more traditional artists who are dithering: men who make concrete block sculptures; painters and ceramicists who feel imposed upon by her request. Traditionalists. Maybe the more experimental the work is, the more it requires all of this stuff, this administration, to support it—to exist, even. A few artists have refused to participate altogether, boycotting the Open Studios in childish protest: the very idea of their private spaces being seen by the public!

And then there is Kieran. He keeps a low profile. Avoiding the meetings, neither defiant nor compliant. A mystery. Into this void Connie's imagination runs wild. Although Pamela's story unsettles her, she can't help but be fascinated by him. His disregard for others, his nihilism. What is it like not to care about what people think, to not feel responsible for anything or anybody? To act instead with total abandon and self-interest, to move through the world like you own it, taking what you want, living without fear?

Outside, the rain gains momentum, slickening the white ceramic bricks of the courtyard wall. Jim's studio windows are open wide in a yawn. No sign of movement. He won't like that, the rain flooding in. Which reminds her: the roof. On a recent walk round, she'd identified an area of weakness in the weather proofing, a potential breach in Tower Street's perimeter. The last thing she needs is a leak and the complaint that would follow, or the roof's potential collapse. Like the images of fire consuming her thoughts on restless nights, water also has the power to destroy. She turns back to the desk and stares at the cork board with its recent clippings from the Hackney Gazette. Reports of deaths: pensioners dying alone in their flats, lying undiscovered for weeks, the wireless droning on. She'd imagined their bodies curled up like those at Pompeii. Why is she so preoccupied with the misery of lonely people? Enough. Now is not the time: the roof can't wait.

The goods lift groans as it edges upwards, carving a channel through the building's floors. Connie stuffs her hands into the pockets of her overalls, letting her body sway slightly with the lift's movement. She tilts her head back and closes her eyes. She imagines the drains filing with rainwater, the sewer levels rising. The lift reaches its destination with a loud jolt, breaking her train of thought. She opens her eyes to see a fine dust falling through the mesh of the ceiling. Shafts of hazy light from the lift's single bulb are filled with floating particles. They catch in the back of her throat. She coughs, watching as the dust settles on the floor. She runs her fingers along the tread plate. Gritty, grey, loose hairs, clumps of dirt. She peers more closely at the mesh of the ceiling and sees floorboards above her in the dim light. From these, particles continue to fall. She doesn't know what is up there—an engine room of some kind? She pulls back the metal shutter and hauls open the solid concertina outer door.

She squints through the downpour. A flash of lightning. London's buildings are a smudge on the horizon. She moves quickly to the tender spot, the potential leak, and gingerly feels along the flashing. It had cracked from the heat of the summer, but last week's spot repair will hold, for now. Sopping already, her curiosity wins out and she approaches the engine room. The compact rectangular space juts upwards into the sky from the middle of the roof. On one side a door with an electrical hazard sign reads DANGER OF DEATH. It's padlocked—no signs of forced entry. Behind it there are cogs and cables under tension, mechanisms enabling the lift to move. She relaxes her shoulders and wipes the rain from her face. On the other side of the engine room she sees the outline of a small hatch. Why has she not noticed it before?

She rubs her finger in a dent along its vertical edge, fishing a penknife from her pocket and slotting it carefully into the gap. She levers the blade slightly; the hatch swings open. A cloud of dust whips into the air. She stumbles at the landslide falling to the floor, draining like sand in an hourglass. Fuck. There is so much of it. She grimaces with disgust at the sheer amount of unidentified matter. Years of skin and dirt. The rain will clear it. The hatch is practically empty, nothing of note. Some old tools, bits of rope. An engineer's cupboard, she supposes, a relic from the building's former past. On the inside of the hatch door, a newspaper clipping absorbs water, turning a dark grey, its ink bleeding. Strange it has got this dusty. Has that much time passed? She's sad to see it forgotten. She watches the dust turn into a river of sludge, running towards the gutter as the rain pummels down. She'll come back with a dustpan later once the storm subsides.

For the rest of the afternoon, Connie works in her studio, leaning hunched over the desk. Her body feels fused to the chair as she selects images, cutting and gluing delicate paper fragments. Piles of cigarette ends accumulate in the jam-jar lid she uses as an ashtray. Shifting in her seat, she pulls herself upright, arching her back to stretch it.

Suddenly finding the fug of the room overwhelming, she goes over to the window. The heavy rain continues. The green expanse of the fields is empty of people, but in the street below, Connie is shocked to see the red-haired girl again. She has moved out from under the tree's meagre shelter into the street directly opposite the front door of the studios. She stands, exposed, her face turned to the sky, the rain pounding down.

The girl's pale woollen skirt is saturated with water. It sags and sticks to her thighs. A gabardine coat, also soaking, and far too big, flaps at her sides. The girl doesn't seem to feel it enough to move, but pulls the coat's dripping folds tightly around her. She shifts from foot to foot, rocking her head back, beckoning the onslaught onto her upturned face. She's young—could be as young as fifteen, sixteen. Even in the gloom, her red hair gleams like copper. She'll make herself ill being out in this. Two women wheeling chequered shopping bags hobble past, their grey hair flattened by plastic bonnets, the straps digging into the loose turkey skin of their necks.

They tut at the girl, shaking their shrunken heads. She sticks out her tongue in retort as they pass. Connie smiles. The girl turns her pale face back to the front entrance of the studios, her arms across her stomach, her gaze steady. The rain beats against the windows.

Connie pulls her coat around her shoulders, walking briskly through the courtyard. She opens the entrance gate and calls out across the street:

"Can I help you?"

The girl's eyes meet hers as though pulled from far away. She doesn't reply or move. Connie leaps across the puddles in the road, pulling the collar of her coat up above her head. She stops in front of the girl and grimaces.

"*You're* all wet now," the girl says.

She narrows green, wide-set almond eyes. She speaks confidently, downy hair above her top lip. No bag or jewellery. Just the clothes she's standing in.

"So are you," Connie replies.

"Yes, but I don't mind."

She looks past Connie, eyes darting back and forth over Tower Street's windows. She's trying hard to disguise her accent, putting on her best telephone voice, but Connie can tell she's from around here: Hackney.

"Are you waiting for someone?" Connie asks, trying to follow the direction of her gaze.

The girl opens her mouth and closes it again.

"You're Connie, aren't you?"

The girl smiles. Her teeth are small with tiny gaps between, like milk teeth.

"Sorry, have we met?" Connie says.

"No, silly. He told me about you."

Connie pauses, unsure how to respond. Smiling back, she says, "All good things I hope."

The girl looks at her with disinterest.

"What's your name?" Connie says, still holding her coat above her head. The downside to this is that the rain flows freely down the sleeves of her shirt, pooling at her elbows.

She tries again. "Are you looking for someone?"

"Sort of. But I know he's gone."

"You want to wait inside?"

The girl is worrying her hands, interlacing her fingers mechanically.

"Do you want a cup of tea? I live just there," Connie says, gesturing to her flat with a tilt of her chin. She wants to get her out of the rain. Talk to her. She reaches for her arm, the girl flinches and binds her body tighter with her coat. There's something wrong. The girl is holding herself uncomfortably, as though she's hiding something.

"Or a biscuit? I've got some Penguins."

"It's not fair, is it? How things work."

"How do you mean?"

"I know what it's like in there," she says, gesturing at the building.

They both stare up at Tower Street's blank façade.

"Can I call someone for you?" Connie asks.

"I can take care of myself. How old are you anyway?" the girl says.

"Twenty-two. How old are you?"

She pauses. "Do you like being an artist?"

"I'm not an artist."

"What are you then?"

"I don't know what I am."

"Neither do I," says the girl, looking down at her feet. "Anyway, *I* won't be living in Hackney when *I'm* twenty-two."

"Oh yeah? Where will you be living?"

"Who knows. Maybe Mozambique? Or the Bahamas? At school there are girls who don't know where Hyde Park is, can you believe that? I've been all over London."

"I like to walk around the city too."

"Do you?" the girl replies suspiciously. "Where do you go?"

"Around the East End, mostly."

"Not here!" she wails. "God, it's hideous. Do you have a camera?"

"Yes."

"Is it a Pentax or Leica?"

"A Leica," Connie answers, taken aback by the girl's knowledge. "Do you like photography?"

"Leica's are ladies' cameras."

"Who told you that?"

"Never you mind."

"People don't like women having cameras," Connie says. "You should see the looks I get."

"I'm used to getting nasty looks," the girl says.

"I've got mine in my studio—why don't we have a cup of tea and a biscuit, and you can have a go with it?"

"No," the girl replies, firmly.

Before Connie can respond, the girl flashes her a weak smile and stumbles away towards Mare Street, her shoes squelching. Connie watches her, a slight waddle in her gait, as though she's carrying something heavy. The girl reaches the corner with her head bowed and shoulders rounded against the weather. She looks back at Connie and the building and shouts, "What goes in must come out! That's the thing they don't tell you. There's no other way. It has to come out somehow!" She turns and breaks into a run, her figure blurring in the deluge of the afternoon.

Back in her flat, a puddle forms on the linoleum at Connie's feet. *It has to come out somehow.* What did she mean? Connie feels shaken by the exchange. Most of the time the artists keep themselves to themselves. Many live elsewhere: Notting Hill, Archway, Hampstead. The few who stay on site often never leave, only scuttling off to Cork Street openings or late-night dancing. They have little contact with the people around these streets. A city within a city. The encounter was a reminder: this is someone else's patch.

The girl's words confused her. How did she know about photography? And "Leica's are ladies' cameras" wasn't her speaking: someone else had said that. The "he" is worrying her. Connie's head grows hot. She hates being the topic of some stranger's conversation. Who was talking about her? She feels vulnerable. Anyway, so some sad bloke in the studios is fooling around with a girl half his age—so what? Nothing new there. But the girl was very young, and she seemed, well... unhinged.

She hangs her coat over the back of a chair and positions it in front of her heater. Unpeeling her jumper, jeans, socks and pants, she plonks them in a soggy pile by the door. From her bed she pulls a patchwork blanket around her. She hasn't kept many of Harold's things, but she is grateful for the pink slipper bath: an enamelled oyster clam stuck to a circular base, chipped around the rim and worn in the seat from the rubbing of many bums. She fills the kettle, lights the stove and waits, shivering, for the water to boil. She chews her fingernails.

Maybe it's good to learn things the hard way—don't we all have to? She thinks about her childhood. Suburban Crawley was so different to Hackney, but maybe it's all the same to a teenage girl. The men Connie was with were the ones who pursued her; she had no time to think about what she wanted, who *she* might pursue. Her encounters were defined by the desires of men. Limited roles available. She thinks of the squeaking pleather seats of a Hillman Imp...

The kettle squeals and she turns off the gas and pours the water into the bath. Steam rises from the shallow puddle. She fills the kettle again and pours. She clambers in, folding her legs into her chest and scooping palmfuls of warm water over her goose-pimpled skin. She reaches from the bath, stretching to retrieve her tattered notepad from the kitchen counter. She flicks back through her notes, lists, reminders. Back in January there'd been the attempted break in, so maybe the girl was scouting the place out for someone? No. The girl was too lost in her own thoughts, too distracted, not alert. Also, she wasn't trying to hide—she was brazen; she wanted to be seen. Connie should have pushed harder, asked more questions. She had been wrong-footed—sensed something threatening, even. She needs to find out who the girl is, *and* who the man is.

Dry now in long johns and an old jumper, wet clothes steaming in front of the gas heater, Connie scrawls notes in her pad: *Photographers/Artists who use Photography. Any artists who have local connections? Check Index.* She resolves to do more rounds of the building; she has let things at Tower Street slip, become too distracted with her artwork. She looks down at the evidence of her absence: stacks of paper in dishevelled piles across the desk, half-drunk mugs of cold tea and fag ends framing the typewriter. She picks up the pages she collected from Kieran a few days ago. She had been surprised how many artists had chosen to use a portrait of themselves rather than a picture of their work in the catalogue; she had not been surprised by how flattering most of these head shots were. Kieran's photograph, however, shows a painting—a sheer surface of hard-edged vertical stripes. A picture of control, precision, execution. *Smithey, K.* She files his papers.

  Although she hadn't admitted it to Pamela, she has mixed feelings about the Open Studios—she is excited and also nervous about people seeing her work. She's conscious of the fact that most of the artists think of her as a busybody, an organiser—not a proper artist like them. Standing in front of a trestle table, she takes paper, glue and other bits of stationery from her bag, having lifted them from the office earlier that day. It isn't stealing; it's redistribution. Despite lacking confidence, she's pleased with her new collage, it's coming along nicely. She flicks through an old manual for eye examinations bought on a stall at the Waste, past the butcher's and the eels. The men there exist on a sliding scale of wealth; the further down the road you go the less there is to buy. The loneliest among them sell a single watch, wireless, suit, or maybe a stack of long-playing records, cigarettes welded to their stained fingers.

The fragments of paper fanned out in front of her are mostly more tales of woe. A man beating his wife to death with a hammer, the headline for the article reading: "Husband's Tragic Story of Torment and Deceit". The story has affected her—how was it, she had asked herself, that one minute a man can be making his morning tea, throwing out the leaves on the earth around his dahlia plant, and the next, grabbing a hammer from the bushes, going inside and without a thought—brain as empty as his china cup— beating his wife's head in? No premeditation, apparently. The jury let him off. The man walked free because "he loved her very much". She shudders.

Connie picks up a copy of *NOVA* magazine from the top of her pile. She's always coveted its glossy pages, wanted to be the new kind of woman its tag line describes. The cover is emblazoned with a colour photograph featuring three female models chained to the steel bars of a gate: lilac eyes and crimped hair, otherworldly faces pouting. The words "Remembering May '68" vibrate in red bubble writing. She remembers *her* May '68, learning shorthand and losing her temper with the ink ribbon on a typewriter. Most of the girls she sat next to would be married now, probably have children. Their futures were mapped out like quarterly budget forecasts. She flips to the cover feature. Photographs of students, their raised arms wielding painted banners. Heads dodging police batons, cars upturned in the streets. The last page focuses on the aftermath of the protests in Paris. Among the images is a group photograph: trade unionists outside a factory building. Squinting in disbelief, she realises she knows a face in the crowd. How strange. His sideburns are longer, and the hair cut is shorter, but those eyes, the intensity… She's certain it's Kieran. She scrutinises the image for a moment longer before checking the caption: a list of names from left to right. "Kelly" instead of Kieran and "Sweeney" instead of Smithey. *What?* Probably just a mistake. She pauses. Something about the similarity in the names: too wrong to be a copywriting error, but too right to be a different person. Who was Kelly Sweeney? For that matter, who was Kieran Smithey?

The next day

Outsiders in the studio. People of non-artistic origin. Jim hadn't liked the idea at first. The thought of all those bodies moving through his corridors, bits of their skin mingling with those of the residents. All their stupid questions about how long things took to make or why this colour and not that one. Bemused faces. The English has always been so anti-intellectual. He had thought again. He would have a ready-made audience for his dust cupboard. He could take photographs, mock things up as though it were a private view. It didn't matter that they were nobodies, plebs off the street. Finally, he'd get the exposure he deserved.

Water pools on the bitumen from yesterday's storm. There is a clarity to the air now, a lightness. The attention he anticipates feeds the garden of his mind: soon there could be critical articles, buyers, maybe even awards. He imagines his retrospective: rooms of abstract prints transitioning into grand spaces filled with documentation of his architectural sculptures, the outside pulled in. Perhaps he will create a site-specific response to the gallery itself… Museums have many hands and generous resources.

Energy in the tips of his fingers. Full breaths deep in his lungs. Happiness blooming. In the fields below, a group of men play cricket, their white bodies bobbing and darting on the green like snowdrops whipped by the wind. He has never understood the game. Team sports have always been an activity to negotiate. The curse of being an only child. Enough daydreaming—it's time to get on. There are chores to be completed: a visit to the bank, picking up food supplies. Maybe he'll get a haircut, his first in two years. He needs to look his best.

Instantly he knows something is wrong. Something has changed. He stumbles, water from the puddle seeps into the cracked soles of his boots. Soggy, uneven piles of dust spatter the patch of roof directly below the cupboard. His hands are at the hatch before he can articulate any thoughts. The door swings open. Did he forget to close it? He doubles over, as though the wind has been knocked out of him, as though a cricket ball has pounded him in the gullet. All that was blooming in his chest is gone in an instant, shrivelled, wiped away just like all his beautiful work. There is nothing. Nothing. He looks around frantically, hopelessly. His hands touch the previously submerged objects. There is the rope; there, the wrench. He tries to shield them from the elements. He feels violated. A distant pop of leather hitting wood. Cries from the field. Dazed, he spins away from the empty cupboard and collapses on a deckchair. It would take him months to recreate. Months. He will miss the Open Studios; the opportunity is gone. He reaches into his pocket for a smoke. "Fuck!" he shouts. It's the first word he's said all day. As he fumbles for matches, he sees it. The red fire bucket for cigarette butts. Next to the bucket, a dustpan and brush. His mind races. So neatly swept. Someone has taken their time, given the task their attention. There's only one person in this building who cleans like that: Connie.

Congenital abnormalities affect the intrauterine body and are noticeable at birth. These hardenings or misshapings happen during gestation before the owner in possession of these defects has taken an independent breath. Developmental disorders are similar but become apparent sometime after birth. They wait. Gene defects, inherited disorders, the by-products of a sickness passed by the host. All these failures are defined by their appearance: dysplasia (abnormal), aplasia (absence), hypoplasia (underdevelopment) and hyperplasia (overdevelopment). Plasia, *the Latin for development, is from the Greek* plasis *meaning "moulding or formation".*

10 June 2017

The digital display on the cooker flashes 11:56 am. Already? I move through the assault course of boxes, swinging the tote bag of bread and coffee onto the kitchen island's granite surface with a thump. No signs of life upstairs. The flat is silent, the still air stifling. Fuck's sake, I thought if I went out for some nice things, she'd at least meet me halfway. Unscrewing the stiff Moka coffeemaker, I take out the perforated metal basket and blow the compacted grounds into the bin, a trick I learnt from a Bolognian chef. I dig a plastic scoop into the bag of Allpress and fill the now empty chamber with fresh, blackcurrant-scented coffee.

My grey toolbox is behind the ironing board. Its battered lid opens to reveal trays of my tools: mostly inherited from Grandad, a few gifts and bits I've bought myself. "I'm starting," I shout. I take out a hammer and a three-quarter inch bolster, tapping its smooth handle against my lower lip. I consider the wall. The cool surface is slightly textured under my hand. When you've got an animal on the block, before the primal cuts, before the body is divided into meat, it's still whole, still a creature, just about. There's integrity in that wholeness.

I dig a corner of the tool into the wall and give the butt a few taps. I feel the tension in my shoulders and neck release. When you break an animal down into joints, there's always a moment when you worry you might ruin it. A split second before your muscle memory kicks in, and confidence returns. The layers chip away easily, flaking like dead skin onto the floorboards. The brick underneath is soft and dry; the plaster is chalky; I sneeze. It's easy, mindless work this, the kind I enjoy, like chopping mountains of peppers for sofrito or shelling peas. Productive. How work should feel.

The dust coats the oiled brown floorboards like icing sugar sieved across a tray of frangipane.

I paw across the cardboard boxes leaving white handprints, until eventually, I find the bundle of decorator's polythene. Kneeling at the foot of the wall, I unfold the flimsy sheeting and tape it along the skirting. Swiping away the settled powder, I find that two boards shift under the pressure of my hand. Tentatively I prod them again, fingering their splintered edges. They look out of place. They don't fit neatly into the rest of the boards. I put my face to the floor, trying to peer into the gap. I read an article once about a builder finding Nazi gold while renovating a bungalow. Imagine. Or there could be a "rat king": a bundle of squirming rodents, bound together by their entwined tails. I jam the tip of the bolster into the gap and prise at the board. It lifts.

I push my fingertips under one edge, trying not to splinter or damage the floor around it. There is something. There's a gaping hole in the floor and something is buried in it. It looks like rags tucked between the joists. Upstairs the toilet flushes and I scramble to my feet. I strain to hear the direction of Tam's shuffling footsteps. They get quieter. She's going back to bed. I look at the hole. I've too much to do. I need to be focussed—it's probably nothing anyway. A stiff bundle, about the size of a small tin loaf. Layers of ash-like dust, hair and dark grains of mouse shit have settled over its surface. Gross. I feel suddenly aware of Tam upstairs; I'm protective of my discovery. I keep going. I move quickly, grabbing a pair of marigolds from the cupboard beneath the sink. Gloved and sweating, I straddle the cavity at the base of the wall, cupping my hands under the bundle, agitating it gently. I wince. It's not that I'm squeamish. It's just that I don't like dirt. As a child I'd cry if I got any on my clothes, like I'd spoilt myself. I like things to be clean. Silt falls onto the plastic sheeting as I tilt the bundle up and out, moving it onto the kitchen counter. Whatever it is, it's much lighter than I predicted; it feels hollow. My nose wrinkles at the musty smell.

The rags are actually torn bits of towelling, with smears of what looks like paint, coarse brush marks of green and blue, visible in the terrycloth. The colours have faded; it's old, really old. It gives slightly under the pressure of my fingers, but not softly like fruit—it's tougher than that, more like leather. The outer rags feel brittle, stuck to themselves. I work one corner gently. It resists. I try with more force. I don't want to damage it; I just want to see what it is. I use both hands to lift the towel at one edge, and it makes a dull tearing sound. Underneath it is another layer, finer than the first, protected from the dirt. Cotton canvas, neatly wrapped, swaddling. I spread the outer layer of rags out fully on the counter. It's suddenly clear why the fabric's all stuck together. The canvas core is covered in irregular crimson stains, each long, dried blot the size of a peony in bloom.

13 September 1975, the Night

Connie stands in front of the bedroom mirror and manoeuvres her right tit into the black bra. The lace fabric is cold and damp after a month being mangled between her mattress and the studio wall, discarded in the throes of a promising but disappointing liaison. The streetlamp casts an orange glow into her bedroom. She considers her reflection. Lean like a teenage boy. No significant identifying marks aside from the long thin scar on her right foot where, as a baby, she'd had the bone of a sixth toe removed. She wishes the surgeon had left it. Her dark hair is frizzy and tied back with a rubber band. She doesn't look at herself like this often, since most days she can ignore her body, smothered as it usually is in baggy overalls. In the kitchen she wets a flannel under the tap and rubs it under her armpits, cold water dripping down her sides. She can't be bothered boiling the kettle for hot water. Back in the bedroom she pours red wine into a chipped mug.

It's too early to be getting ready really, but she's too nervous to focus on anything else. Parties in the basement get wild and she doesn't feel up to it. The last party of the summer, Arlo and Des said, one last blowout before the Open Studios, before the cold sets in. They don't usually get under way until after eleven, and it is only eight: three hours stretch ahead of her. She can feel the anticipation vibrating through the building, the stillness occasionally broken by distant swinging doors and rushing footsteps. Only yesterday, Arlo had threatened Connie with spectacles of nudity and pain, cackling as he hauled a drum machine down the basement stairs. Connie had tried to appear tough and unfazed, but they'd sensed her anxiety, seemed to take pleasure in it.

Connie stares at her face in the mirror, two creases carved between her brows like speech marks. Frown lines. She licks her fingers and smooths her bristling eyebrows with firm movements. She doesn't usually wear makeup, but Pamela has given her some old pans of eyeshadow having declared herself too old for it. She picks up a lush, brooding shade called Green Smoke and strokes it with gentle pressure along her lash lines. Next, she rubs a cracked silver eye shadow called Plunge, the colour of tinfoil, deep into her sockets. Harold's wife June always had beautiful makeup. Connie only met her once, during the handover—Harold wasting everyone's time by removing his collection of wacky keyrings from the bundle of caretaker keys, pontificating about each one like a spoilt child. She can remember, distinctly, June's bottle-green nails, her eyebrows plucked completely clean of hair, giving her face a skeletal look.

Connie juts her chin forwards and runs her tongue around the inside of her mouth to inspect a prickling of blackheads at the edges of her lips, like a dirty liner. *It's OK*, people don't look that close. Removing the rubber band, she tries to tame her hair, the thatch responding momentarily to her cajoling before unwinding lazily to settle at various angles around her shoulders. She grabs a smouldering cigarette from the ashtray and inhales deeply.

It's OK, just as long as no one dies tonight. Connie doesn't have anything against people getting high just as long as they keep themselves together. She smokes grass with Pamela sometimes, but only after they finish working. Pamela says she doesn't like how it clouds her head; she doesn't trust her ideas. Connie has taken purple hearts at gigs a couple of times with her ex. She tried mushrooms on the solstice in Dorset last summer, lying next to her friend and feeling the warm grass sprouting through her outstretched limbs. She's also done cocaine. She first tried it during a weekend in Paris. Eighteen, and her first trip abroad. As she and Heather, her friend from secretarial college, wandered through the Louvre, bored and underwhelmed, a short man with grease-slicked hair and a creased navy suit had approached them. They didn't have any money and only the sweaty hostel dorm to go to. It hadn't taken much persuasion to get them to spend the evening with him. Sitting on the metal chairs at a pavement café in Saint-Germain-des-Prés, he had pulled out an ivory vial dangling from a chain nestled in the thick hair of his chest. He coaxed their noses onto the silver tip of its tiny spoon. "Ah, *mes amis*," he'd purred, and encouraged them to lick the white dust from their fingers. That first rush of blood. The desire to smoke endlessly. Her interest in the world growing wayward like a feral cat. As the man went inside to pay, they escaped, flinging napkins across discarded plates of chocolate gateaux, running through the cobbled streets, laughing and panting, reeling at their own power.

No one does cocaine here. Acid is the thing. On her late-night rounds, she sometimes encounters people tripping, lost in the maze of corridors, their pupils dilated. To lose control like that scares her.

Connie touches the turntable needle to the record. A crackle, a drumbeat and the eager, thrumming guitar of Marc Bolan. She finds her indigo flares turned inside-out under the clothes rail and pulls on a crochet vest. The black lace bra is visible behind the sparse woollen lattice. It'll do, she decides, shrugging, and pours herself another mug of wine. Two and a half hours to go.

"Welcome to the plague pit," Des shouts at Connie, smirking, her fingers clasped around the doorframe. Connie opens her mouth to respond, inhaling a hot gust of fag smoke. Before the words come out, Des slinks back through the crowd, laughing. The music is loud, the mood expectant. Overhead, bare bulbs dimmed by red filters dangle, giving the room an aura of warm doom. Arlo and Des painted the walls black immediately after moving in and they absorb all the light. Barely visible on the surface are scribblings in white chalk: "Thee in control of thee" and "quim". People push past as Connie stumbles across the threshold and into the basement. The party hasn't yet reached capacity, but it feels like it might be a big one. An empty PVC gimp suit hangs loosely, its zippered mouth gaping at her from a damp corner. She brushes past oily latex and teetering stacks of porn magazines. A raised wooden platform, makeshift, sits in the middle of the room, with space around it cleared as a dancefloor.

She can see Des's profile spotlit through a crowd of bobbing heads, her chin jutting, a cigarette between her lips. Its cherry jitters like a wasp. Her bandmate Charlie stands beside her, stooping over a synthesiser and a nest of cables with focussed intent, the curly hair hanging over his eyes already wet with sweat. Des vibrates with amphetamine energy, her eyes darting, challenging the crowd. The room trembles with a droning beat. Connie finds a wall and leans against it. She rolls a cigarette, her elbows digging into the cold brickwork.

People's chatter is disjointed, superficial. She watches the room as she smokes. Against the walls are two sofas, bodies squeezed onto them, white fluff poking through their torn stitching. Connie recognises Rosalia, an Argentinean artist, sitting quietly, wedged between two friends who converse behind her back. An ashtray has been upturned into the pot of a cheese plant, and Rosalia fingers the butts into the soil, pushing each one slowly under, flicking the earth from her fingertips before proceeding to the next.

For Connie, these parties promise so much, but deliver little besides a lingering sense of dread and a latent anxiety that some sort of building-related issue will unfold. She needs to stay alert, just in case. She makes her way to the other sofa, one corner of which is free. Oblivious to her presence, a group of three men huddle on the end like vultures. The only one Connie knows is Harold. Back on her first day, during her introductory walk round of the building, he had described a ritual he performed called "the shitting". To Connie's disbelief, he had demonstrated it, marching her towards the stall and standing in the open doorway. Looking her dead in the eyes he'd gone through the whole process. First, he must check for flies or bugs in the water; next he must take sheets of paper and place individual squares around the seat so as to ensure his bottom did not touch it. He called this "preparing the toilet with papers". Tonight, Harold is in full flow.

"I want to make work about life! Not aesthetics and colour," Harold is saying to the other two men.

"But Harold, painting keeps me sane!" one of the other men responds, frustrated, hitting his pudgy fists on the arm of the sofa.

"I understand that," Harold says, reassuringly.

"I wouldn't normally tell anyone this, Harold, but when I'm painting, I'm getting into a sort of ritual," the third man confesses.

"Yes, yes—exactly, exactly. That's it!" Harold replies, excited. All three are gesticulating wildly, their heads— inches apart—poised in a triangle of mutual cock respect.

A pair of legs blocks her view. Jim. "I'm glad I caught you here," he says.

She knows what is coming. "Look, I know no one's been to see you about the leak, Jim, and I'm sorry about that. I have passed it onto management."

"What?" Jim looks confused, angry.

Connie stifles a smile. "How can I help?"

"You owe me an apology." There is real pain in his voice.

"Jim, can't this wait? I'm trying to have some fun for once."

Jim's eyes flare with anger at her dismissal. She hasn't seen him like this before.

"Boy, oh boy, Jim! How are you?" Harold shouts, ignoring Connie.

He lurches forward and grabs Jim by the back of his trousers, pulling him down to the sofa. Jim, startled, tries to wriggle free. Connie takes advantage of the distraction and makes a break for the door. She goes in search of Tower Street's highest point: the roof. She needs its perspective now.

Connie barges the door open with her shoulder. A balmy gust of air as she steps out onto the roof. Past the empty beer bottles, a fraying sun hat. Her bare skin prickles. London Fields is an empty swathe of black; a tiny speckling of streetlamps lines Broadway Market beyond. The distant blare of horns and passing cars sound from Mare Street; the usual buses are shunting along Bethnal Green Road. She feels safe up here. The night conceals nothing, as far as she's concerned—the city, so far away from the East End, is of little significance. When did she last go there? She can't remember. Hackney and Stepney have become her dank little world. She takes another swig of gin from the flask, pulling her tobacco out of her pocket. She'll do a walk round after this cigarette and check all the exits. That'll help her feel more in control. From the basement comes a low thrum. She sucks at her cigarette. God, she loves smoking.

"I thought you might be here," his voice cuts through the air.

Connie turns sharply as Jim lumbers out onto the roof.

"Oh, Jim, give it a break."

"Having fun?" he sneers, his body a silhouette against the light of the doorway.

"Well, I'm trying to."

He takes a swig from a bottle of beer and clears his throat.

She sighs, turning back to look at the fields. She's too tired for Jim's nonsense.

"Why did you do it?" His voice is smaller now, as though grief-stricken.

"What?" She turns to look at him again.

"You know what I'm talking about."

"No, I don't actually."

"My work, the project!"

He throws the bottle towards the lift shaft, and it smashes against the brick, sending fragments of glass skidding.

She cries out.

He stumbles towards her, eyes wild. "It took months to collect all that dust, Connie, months."

She steps back and then stops, conscious again of the roof's edge.

"Wait, what?" she says, her mind racing.

"If you knew anything about art, you'd have understood what I was trying to do."

She stares at the streaks of beer dripping down the lift shaft, the puddle frothing at the base.

"Oh, Jim," she says, her shoulders dropping in sudden realisation. "That was you!" She gestures towards the hatch, remembering the shower of dust, the rain coming down.

Jim shakes his head. "It was a durational project and now you've ruined it."

"I had no idea. It was an accident."

"Ignorant!" he stutters and then closes his mouth again.

"Look, I'm sorry, I really am."

He's blocking her exit.

A silence falls between them. He looks at his feet, crestfallen.

"I need to get on with my walk round..." she says, her voice trailing off. "I'm sorry."

As she reaches the doorway, he calls after her, "I'm watching you, Connie."

She walks quickly through the third floor, eager to get some distance. Despite being deserted, all the lights are turned on. She pulls the cords dangling from the ceiling, re-establishing darkness. As she descends through the building, the sounds from the basement become clearer, the crooning piano, tambourine and ukulele telling her that the cabaret portion of the evening is underway. Everyone will be down there now. On the ground floor she checks the push release bar of the rear fire exit. Secure. She feels shaken. Embarrassed. She needs company. She should go back to the party. She notices at her feet a pattern of circular impressions: the weight of factory table legs, stamped into the floorboards. The circles stare back at her like frightened eyes.

Back in the basement, Pamela sits crossed-legged on a bank of filing cabinets wedged between a paint encrusted sink and a row of small, barred windows running along the basement wall. From this elevated lookout, she has a clear view of the party. Pamela can find the best angles in a room, places where she can see and not be seen. Connie sidesteps Harold and his cronies and picks her way through the bodies swaying around the DIY stage.

"Fancy seeing you here," Pamela yells over the music.

"Did I miss the performance?" Connie asks, grunting as she pulls herself up.

"Not started yet."

"What's taking so long?"

"Arlo had an asthma attack," Pamela replies.

"Shit." Connie pulls a flask of gin from her pocket and takes a swig. "How you doing?" she asks, reaching for Pamela's cigarette and noting her dilated pupils.

"Fine. Still working through some things."

Connie nods. Their weekly enlarging sessions haven't resumed since Pamela returned from America. "How's it going?" she asks.

"I don't know. London feels so small."

This restlessness is new. Connie is reminded there's a lot she doesn't know about Pamela. The music stops suddenly. A harsh white light illuminates the stage, and a smoke machine hisses sharply. The sound of coughing disperses through the crowd. Arlo swaggers towards the microphone and points a Polaroid camera at the audience. A flash of light. The shock of his crooked smile sears across Connie's retina in the afterimage. Wordlessly, Pamela jumps down and moves to the front of the crowd. Caught in the glare of the strobe, her limbs move mechanically.

"How much do you love me?" Arlo bleats.

Sniggers echo through the audience. Long, distorted whines streak from a cornet pressed to Des's lips. The stuttering blips of a guitar riff build steadily to form a rhythm. Bursts of electronic squawks come from the speaker. Arlo, Des and Charlie retreat slowly, and a woman Connie doesn't recognise steps out onto the studio floor, spotlit by a crisp beam. Silence descends. The crowd shuffles and realigns around the new performer. She lies lifeless, a futuristic-looking angel in an ice-blue unitard. It's like the crowd are gathered in mourning to pay their respects. Horns sound: her cue. She starts to move. Slow and controlled, back arching, legs spreading. She sways, not to the beat, but not against it either. Des is in the corner, foot on the FX pedal, hands flexing around the body of a black guitar now, fingers pulling at its strings. If the sounds had material form, they'd be sedimentary rock. The bass is strong and constant; Pressurised air is forced through metal. Waves of higher-frequency frosty synths follow for short bursts, and then retreat.

The woman appears moved by desire; it pulses from her body towards the crowd. Her hips rise upwards and then flop down; she is flat on her back, limp. No money shot, no climax. It's erotic to watch a body be moved by music. Des rocks slightly to keep the rhythm, to keep the beat. She speaks flatly into the microphone: "Beaded, jointed, nipple, replacement, phosphorus, calcium, salt, rust, sub, revolve, hydraulic, mechanism." Her mantra fills the air like fuel vapours from industrial machinery. A brown stain grows in the centre of the woman's kneecap, the blood rushing to form bruises underneath her skin. Connie scans the crowd momentarily; they appear transfixed, moving slowly towards the performer. She's unresponsive. She seems possessed. Connie thinks of physical things crumbling and glitching, tectonic plates shifting, buildings falling. The sound of echoing gunshots, or an amplified metronome, fills the space. Her hips buck up and down in acknowledgment of these reverberations. The crowd begins to close in. Connie feels panic rising. Figures restrict her view. The windows have bars on them. The door is on the other side of the room. She can't breathe. The sound from the stage recedes. The room is disappearing. Spit pools in the corners of her mouth; she swallows; her mouth floods again. The bitter taste of gin is coating her tongue.

Out. *Everything out.*

It was a moment of deep letting go. Of draining, of shedding, of liquids meeting solids, slick and viscous and soaking into dusty planks which sucked—*how they sucked*—as though thirsty.

And yet, it was also a moment of hiding, of locked-up potential buried under wood and among old bobbin heads and reels of thread, in the dark underside places which don't see the light. The kind of items dropped years before by skilled but distracted hands, the hands of those with thick mascara lashes and lined pink lips. Hairnets pinching. No doubt they were dreaming of their own escape at the end of a shift and the drinks down the pub or the weekly bath or whatever else it was young girls being wooed busied their minds with then.

Plenty of blood let here before. Nothing we don't know in our fibres, know in our shale. Not a shock in that sense. Arms mangled between rollers, minced by interlocking metal teeth. Machines made light work of their soft bodies.

Feeling life evaporate within us triggered a memory, of London yellows and Essex reds flying in the air, the seams of mortar, which had once held them close and tight, shattered in a hot instant. How our destroyed neighbours rained down upon us, coating parked cars and dank pavements, clogging drains and smothering saplings in their dusty confetti. Petrol stench and a siren.

The city can, like a crowd, be considered a living entity; its complex processes can be modelled and predicted with a great deal of accuracy and usefulness. Moments of revelation swiftly countered by secrets.

She had come to us for safety, as their kind are wont to do. Stumbling through the streets, the fields. Tonight, we cannot provide it. How this spent little body collapses. Utterly wasted, limp with expended effort. We wait for another alarm to be raised, a new one, but nothing comes. Where we sense emergency there is only an empty calm.

The way they crouched in a corner, eyes popping. She, poleaxed, pelvis straining; he, in awe. Taking it all in, devouring it. He, pushing ripped rags into her mouth, stuffing the cavity—absorbing her whimpers that were like spilled paint. He put on the record player, but she would not be hushed. Not tonight. How she shook. Soft heels: barely walked on stone or gravel or grass, still new. They dug down, pressed down into our boards, and their energy moved us deep into the fibres of our being, through the holes left by worms and even animating the core of us, our steel girders. Then she lost her dimples.

The pressure in the way a back arches, and the legs spread. But although it felt like an explosion, not a squeak or a drop of sweat or blood reached three floors down. We were surprised. She, reeling, not knowing whether it was night or day. Snap back a shiny conker, cracked, sprouting black hair. And his grip, so slight, but true. We know. As though unscrewing a bottle top. We, the building, know what he did.

He always thinks of himself as lucky. A lucky person had the foresight to put paper down. No, wait—that was good sense. But getting it down before the blood? *That* was lucky. Not a drop! The wood feels damp; the ammonia makes his eyes sting. It'll pass. His whole body vibrates. He spins around instinctively. *Ha!* There's no one there; he needs to relax. He opens the window, inhaling sharply through his nostrils, filling his lungs. Breathing, still breathing. He almost wishes he could stay. Painting in here would be a trip. He isn't a religious man, but he believes in certain energies.

It's a common misunderstanding that all blood squirts. Sometimes it does if you do real damage—if you nick an artery. More often, it's like a tap left running, just gently oozing. Seeing blood drain out of a person makes you wonder how a body could ever contain it in the first place. He takes one last look and then nudges the edge of the plank into the recess at the base of the wall, letting it down gently, smoothing the floorboard flush with a few knocks of his fist at each corner.

He wouldn't say he feels powerful. More than anything, he feels surprised by his instincts. When it was screaming like that. He'd held it in his hands, and watched it try to breathe. A mouth full of gunk that he hadn't bothered to empty. Simple. Yes. She would think back on this and thank him. Eyes spinning in her skull; she hadn't known a thing. He pats the roll of film in the top pocket of his jacket. It's going to be a corker. It was the only thing to do in a situation like that. It really was her finest performance. He'd miss her. One day he'd look her up. Maybe.

The timing was lucky too. A party! Of all the nights. He shakes his head in disbelief. He leans on the sink. Who would people believe anyway? It doesn't matter. She doesn't matter. His hands had been shaking. The feeling of holding a dead weight. A wave of energy had rippled through him.

Outside the sky is a deep Payne's grey. It's not morning yet. The pulsing sounds of the party are audible still, carried through the open window. He will need to be careful avoiding the last dregs. He's not tired; he's ready. Tapping the floorboards with a bare foot, he realises he didn't even look to see if it was a boy or a girl. He pauses. No, the mess isn't worth it. Who cares? And he needs to get packing. He's used to going lightly, not leaving a trace. This time it had been close.

He's learnt a valuable lesson, but it's time to move on. He can settle wherever; he knows how to build things, and he isn't workshy. Artists getting comfortable in cosy studio set ups: not his thing. Women nosing in his business? Fuck off. It had only ever been somewhere to lay his head. Besides, the street is as good a studio as any; he's always told people that. He needs to be amongst it, out there—in *real life*. Otherwise, you go soft. It'll be nice to get a bit of distance from this lot. He hates all the talk. He has always been interested in experiences, in confronting the actual thing, the moment: paint and skin, pain and flesh, life. He's heard Berlin is entertaining in the spring. Lakes. Museums. Nice girls. This town is dead.

"Connie, you OK?" Mark, the mail artist, asks.

She's crouching unsteadily against the wall in the basement passage, her head between her knees. She looks up to see a puddle of water forming at Mark's feet.

"Why are you dripping?" she asks.

"I had to make a point."

"Huh?" she pants, the nausea subsiding.

"I've been banned from the pub for not washing, so I came back to take a photograph of myself having a bath."

"Fully clothed?" she says, smiling weakly.

"They didn't stipulate!" He waves an outstretched arm in her face, a Polaroid between his fingers. "Proof!"

"Help me up…" she says.

He takes her hand and she stands unsteadily.

"Is the performance still going on?" she asks.

"I think it just finished. What's happened?"

A crowd spills out into the passage, and new arrivals descend the basement steps. Connie collapses into Mark; bodies jostle around them as they squirm and fight for a way out. Pulled in opposite directions by the throng, they're separated, and she finds herself released into the bunker, a pitch-black windowless space. Tower Street's ground zero. Usually the home of Circuit and their kinetic assemblages, tonight it is serving an alternative purpose. Low funk guitar and Jane Birkin's dulcet tones come from the record player. The smell of Palo Santo. For a second, she panics, but free from the fraught closeness of the passage, she relaxes. She breathes into the dark, safe in the knowledge she can't be seen. She steps forward. Waits. Fingers gently intertwine with hers. She lets them pull her deeper in.

Sometime later, Connie emerges from the bunker through the back basement stairwell. This side of the building—the side closest to the railway line—is quiet. She ties her hair back, wipes her face, adjusts her clothes. Her mouth tastes foreign with the combination of other people's spit. She smiles and looks around shyly, climbing the stairs but passing no one. At the ground floor she makes her way quickly towards the caretaker's flat, laughing to herself as she stumbles through the corridors. So, this is what freedom feels like? She feels powerful, bold.

She kicks the courtyard door open and is faced with Kieran as he slams the entrance gate closed.

"Kieran, hi!" She tries to compose herself.

He stalls, clearing his throat. "Connie."

He doesn't move. He looks agitated; there are beads of sweat across his forehead.

"Everything OK?" she asks.

"Grand. Busy." He wipes his forehead and walks towards her, heading for his studio.

"All work and no play," she replies.

"Something like that." He pushes past her, avoiding eye contact.

New confidence surges through Connie as she follows him into the corridor. "I've been meaning to ask you actually, I wanted to show you something—have you got a minute?"

"Not really," he says, quickening his step.

"Oh, come on," Connie calls after him. "Let your hair down. Pamela thought it was hilarious!"

At this, he stops. "Pamela?" He turns to her, his expression unreadable. "I suppose I could do with a nightcap," he says. He smiles but his eyes are cold.

Stepping in through the door of her flat, she flips on the overhead light. Standing next to Kieran she feels suddenly self-conscious about her things: the poster and scarf tacked jauntily to the wall, the beaded necklaces dangling around her lamp. It all seems childish and affected. He stares at her photographs, both hands in his jean pockets.

"Do you want a drink?" she asks.

"Please."

"It's gin," she replies.

"It'll do. Thanks."

She sets two mugs on the table and pours a generous measure into each. He has an animal energy about him. Alert. He tracks the perimeter of the room slowly, inspecting it. He fondles the corner of the closed curtains as though to remark on the fabric, but instead flicks them apart with two long fingers.

"Looking for someone?" She feels the quick pulse of her heart in her chest.

He turns towards her, smiling again. "So how was the party?"

She holds his gaze and pulls out one of the two chairs from under the table, its legs scraping along the floor. She waits for him to take the seat next to her, but he moves past it and sits on the end of her bed, bouncing gently. The mattress springs wheeze softly under his weight. Seeing him now, captured in the intensity of the overhead lamp, he looks older than she had thought. A network of fine lines spreads out from the corners of his eyes.

"I just popped my head in," she replies. "It's busy down there." She sips her drink.

He reaches for the mug and knocks its contents back in one.

"So, you were working tonight?" she asks.

"You could say that," he replies, still bouncing.

"I wouldn't do that. I made the bed base, not my best work."

"Feels pretty sturdy," he says and shrugs. "What did you want to show me? I haven't got long."

She empties the last of the flask into his cup. "Wait here."

"I don't usually like surprises," he replies, as she races unsteadily up the stairs to her office and rips the *NOVA* cutting from her pinboard.

"So," he says, as she returns. "What is it?" His voice is cold and hard.

She sits back down at the table. "I found this picture of a young Kieran."

He stops bouncing.

"Or should I say Kelly."

The vein in his right temple throbs.

She unfolds the paper and looks at him. "I didn't get it either. This is you, isn't it?" She lays the page on the table, and swallows. He doesn't look at the paper. His dark eyes remain fixed on hers. He darts forward, but she's quicker, and his fingers grasp at nothing, curling into a fist.

"Give that to me," he hisses. He leans on the table, the shadow of his body falling across her face.

"Why?" She hears her own voice, much quieter than she expected. She presses the piece of paper to her chest, her confidence failing.

"I just want to look," he says, calmly.

He reaches his hand down to her face and tucks a few strands of stray hair behind her ear. She smells chemicals—soap and ammonia. She flinches at his touch.

"You get me down here in the middle of the night to see an old picture and then refuse to show me?" He crouches beside her, one arm wrapped around the back of her chair, the other flat on the table across her body, penning her in.

"Or did you want something else?" he asks, quietly. She can hear the menace in his voice. His eyes pass across the holes of her crocheted vest. He moves his hand from the table, pressing it firmly on her thigh.

"Get off me," she says.

"Give me the picture," he threatens, his grip tightening.

She flings it away from her.

He dives desperately, scrabbling for the scrap of paper. Righting himself, Kieran flicks his hair.

"Always preferred Kelly. More unusual for a man. I won't go into that now, another time maybe." He moves behind her chair, blocking the exit. "Paris was a riot," he says ruefully. "Can't imagine it would have been your kind of thing. Mayhem in the streets."

Connie's legs are like jelly. He brushes her hair to one side, stroking her exposed shoulder blade.

"It's a shame to be in your bedroom under these circumstances."

He's breathing hard. Connie's hands grip the edge of her seat. He moves in front of her, crotch by her face. Fumbling in his pocket, he pulls out a polished steel lighter and sparks the flint, holding the paper to the flame.

"What are you doing?" Connie shouts, jumping to her feet and knocking her chair aside.

He laughs, dropping the blazing ball and stamping on it sharply, grinding charred paper and ash into the linoleum with the toe of his boot.

"What do you mean?" he asks.

"Why did you do that?"

"What?"

"Burn it! The photo—you didn't even look!"

"What photo?" He opens his arms like a magician completing a trick, moving towards her, pushing her against the wall with his body.

She tries to shout but her voice catches in her throat.

A loud knock at the door. "You in there, Connie?"

"Jim!" she calls out.

The front door swings open as Jim blusters into the room, panting.

Kieran steps backwards, knocking into the table; the gin bottle clatters to the floor.

"Well, back to it!" Kieran says, clapping his hands together, the coldness gone from his voice. He sidles past Jim. "You two have a good one," he says.

The morning after

She had slept fitfully, fully clothed and buried under blankets, disturbed by voices and footsteps, doors slamming, people outside on the street. At each sound, she sat up rigid, gripping a pair of scissors for protection. At some point, she'd passed out, the scissors falling from her limp hand to the rug.

Her crusted eyes open, head throbbing, confused with flashing memories from the night before. Her dreams had been full of small, scampering animals—tiny mice, scurrying and curling in cracks and cavities, dying, their bodies disappearing into a deep shag carpet that grew deeper and thicker as if fertilised by their decay.

She gets out of bed, adjusting her clothes, and blunders into the kitchen to put the kettle on. Nescafé, six sugars. Sipping the treacly brew, she massages her temples with one hand. Red wine and gin: a bad combination. Her encounter with Kieran is configured hazily in her mind. Parties escalate things. They are an expulsion of collective tension, the kind built up when sharing space. She stands in the doorway of her bedroom. The footprint is there on the floor: smudges of ash, small scorch marks on the lino. Connie grabs her notepad from the bedside table and falls back on the bed. She flicks through the pages of illegible notes drunkenly scrawled in the early hours, when she was certain Kieran would return. In the cold light of day, she feels relief. She shakes her arms as if shrugging off a shiver, like she's escaped something.

After another cup of coffee, Connie is bundled up in her overalls ready to face the world. It's almost lunchtime, and she feels guilty about wasting the day, dread in the pit of her stomach about what lies beyond the front door.

Whatever has happened, she'll have to deal with it—shoo off the stragglers, close doors, clear mess. She remembers the article Pamela showed her once about an American artist who did cleaning performances. She called them "maintenance works", even wrote a manifesto: *Who's Going to Clean up After the Revolution?* Hands in the pockets of her overalls, Connie knows the answer already.

She listens at the threshold, staring at the hooks on the back of the front door. Quiet. It's as if the studios, like their occupants, are also trying to recover. Sometimes it feels like the buildings take days to get into gear after a big night, as though ashamed by all they have witnessed. Sensitive to their shared, slow revival, Connie vows to move gently. Her headache has subsided, masked now by caffeine. A deep breath. She swings open the door.

First, she sees a ghostly mass of mucus gleaming on the floor of the courtyard, its surface wrinkled with a bluish tinge. Then, she spies a slick of purple fibrous tissue which twirls around the iron railings of the basement stairwell. From this, a bloody trail drips towards Connie's front door before making for the building's entrance where a clot of matter hangs from a spike above the gate, shrivelling in the air. Connie retches, steadying herself against the wall.

She smells the strong, musky odour of fox piss. Animal destruction has a frenzied quality. At the bottom of the basement stairs, she finds the source: two masticated bin bags, their contents scattered. Dried paint tubes, apple cores, tea bags, old food and noxious chemicals, all mingling together. Those agile little fuckers. She grabs a roll of bin bags and some marigolds from the kitchen. But the blood? That's strange. Standing on her tip toes she untangles the clot from the spike. There's a rational explanation for this. She remembers last night's misunderstanding with Jim, the dust work on the roof. Arlo and Des often use offal and blood blagged from the butchers to make their performances more convincing. That's it. She'd missed their full set last

131

night and this is just the remnants. It's a pity they haven't taken better care with the clean-up; she's angry they left it all out to spoil but affected by the impact of their stunt. She bends to rescue one of the punctured bin bags at the foot of the basement steps and its contents spill from a hole the shape of a gurning mouth. The bag slips in her hands, tearing wide open. A wine bottle falls and there's a loud plonk as it bounces off the concrete, skidding towards Circuit's bunker at the end of the passageway. Blood-soaked, soggy matter plops out onto Connie's shoes: fists of tissue and rags soaked in dark red; newspapers wadded up.

"Bollocks! That's *it*," she says under her breath.

The disintegrating bin bag hanging loose in her hand, Connie strides towards Arlo and Des's door. She beats on the wood with the side of her fist.

"Wake up, you lazy gits!" she shouts, her heart pumping.

Muffled voices, a crash, hands fumbling at the bolts. The door creaks ajar to reveal Des in a moth-eaten black silk dressing gown, her eyes puffy, mascara smudged across her cheeks. She squints at Connie.

"Uh hum?" she murmurs, sniffing.

Connie drops the bin bag on the step.

Des shuffles back. "Jesus, what you doing?" Her pupils are big black pennies.

"What the fuck happened here?" Connie asks, gesturing at their feet.

"Uh, that's a heavy flow," Des mumbles, laughing.

"Next time, do a better job of clearing up, Des! You're taking the piss. I'm not your fucking servant," Connie says, gesturing down the passage.

Des looks confused. "What you goin' on about, Con?"

She pulls the gown tighter around her bare chest, and clenches her teeth, trying to stop the grinding of her jaw.

"This stuff—this bloody mess! Chunks of it hanging off the fence! Do you think I'm in the mood? The foxes have thrown it all over the place."

"You *what*?" Des looks genuinely shocked. "Connie, please, my head is raging, OK? Give us a few hours, and I'll help you later, I promise."

She closes the door.

Connie throws the bin bag against the wall. It splatters and drips down the chipped paint. Fine. If they don't care, why should she? They can clear it up. She picks her way back up the steps and through the courtyard, avoiding the bloody rags and a slick of curdled milk. She opens the door to her flat and closes it hard behind her. A mouse's tail vanishes behind a tin of powdered custard on the kitchen shelf. She slides down the back of the door to sit on her haunches, banging her head back in frustration. Anger swirls in her stomach. She's sick of these people. She replays last night's argument with Kieran. The things he said that she'd never be able to prove. The pleasure he seemed to take from her fear. And what if Jim hadn't been there? What might have happened then? She won't stand for it. She's angry he made her feel scared in her own bedroom, and she's angry she can't make him feel like that. She hates how he made Pamela question herself, when she was usually so sure, so confident. How many other women was he doing this to? He has to leave. She has to get him out. This is her building.

She mounts the stairs with purpose. No gentle movements anymore. She and the building need to work together. As she stands at Kieran's door, readying herself to fight, there's a sound at the end of the corridor.

"Not now, Jim, I'm busy," she snaps.

"Looking for Kieran?"

"Yes, I am, actually. Have you seen him?"

"No, but…"

Connie turns back to the door and hammers on it loudly. "Kieran!"

"I think, after he left us, he had a busy night," he murmurs nervously.

"Jim, just leave me to it, will you!" she snaps. Immediately regretting it.

"I'm only trying to help!" he huffs, stomping away.

"Oh, Jim…" she shouts after him, but it's too late, he's gone.

She hammers again, louder. She pulls down hard on the handle, expecting it to be locked, but the door swings open. A thin mattress stands stripped and tipped up against the wall, yellow-ringed splotches across its faded surface. The narrow metal locker for flammable materials, a requirement for all studios, stands erect, empty, its door hanging open. The floorboards look scrubbed clean, and the room smells strongly of chemicals: disinfectant, bleach. A breeze blows in through one of the large open windows. She shivers. A gas heater is disconnected in the corner, its hose neatly coiled. An exposed bulb swings overhead, moved by the breeze.

She walks into the studio and closes the door, snapping the latch closed. Everything is clean, as though recently wiped. She paces along the edge of the room, the floorboards creaking under her feet, and peers into the empty locker. She steps towards the mattress cautiously and pulls it away, letting it fall to the floor with a soft thump. Nothing. No dust or dirt or hair or anything to indicate it had been occupied only the night before. She kicks the wall in frustration. Outside, London Fields stares blankly back. She sits down on one end of the mattress and leans forward, elbows on knees, scanning the room. There are no clues, no traces; nothing to go on. She sighs despondently as exhaustion sets in.

10 June 2017

What is she doing down there? It's not like Jane to be this quiet; normally she throws herself through space, movements soundtracked by bangs and slams. I breathe deeply. In the fields below the ageing hipsters drone on, their chit-chat mixing with the mumbling of tourists, destination diners, sample sale shoppers. The kinds of people who have hours to kill and cash to waste. People like me. A crash downstairs. Swearing. My empty stomach aches. I should probably eat, or at least feign interest in what she brings back. I sit up, the air beyond the duvet feels fresh. The fine hairs on my arms stand on end.

I wait at the top of the spiral staircase, my bare feet cold on the metal treads. From here I have a good view of the open-plan space down below. Jane is hunched over the kitchen island, palms planted on the counter, head bowed. She looks like the general of a defeated army contemplating a final, hopeless manoeuvre. Her shorn head is coated with a fine white dust, giving her a ghostly look. I start to descend; the stairs make a deep sonorous clang under my weight. She reels around.

"Tam!" Her eyes are wide, her shoulders stiff, as she looks up.

"What are you doing?" I ask.

"Just started to strip the wall…" she says, shifting on the spot as I approach. She takes a step towards me, blocking my path to the kitchen island.

There's something behind her, laid out on the granite. Scraps of dirty rags, peeled back like dead petals. Jane tries to steer me away, her hands firmly gripping my elbows. I tense, trying to shake her off.

"What is that?"

"Come and sit down over here."

I wriggle from her grip and twist towards the island, and she lets me go.

There, on the granite, is something small. The skin of it is waxy and shrivelled; it doesn't look real. Bound around its form is a long, black knobbly cord.

"I found it under the floor." Jane's voice is trembling.

"Under the floor?"

"I was going to—I don't know." She looks scared. "It was hidden," she says.

A tiny foot, five miniature toes. An expression of pain preserved on its crumpled face.

"Don't touch it!" Jane shouts, as I move closer. Her hands are shaking.

"It's OK," I say. I feel calm, calmer than I've felt in months.

She starts to circle the table. "Fuck," she murmurs.

It's the umbilical cord, that's what it is.

A new-born baby.

"We need to call the police," I say quietly.

We look at each other. For the first time in months, I feel like I really see her.

"No," she pleads, raising both hands behind her head.

I lean in close to the body. Its face is gnarled like a peach stone.

"It's a crime scene," I continue.

"Crime scene? Stop it. You don't know that—it could have died of natural causes."

"Does it seem natural to hide a baby among your water pipes?"

She opens her mouth to speak but closes it again.

"Don't you want to know what happened?" I ask.

She doesn't reply. We stand there in silence. The rich smell of coffee begins to waft through the room.

"I knew I felt something in here. The pressure. Like something sad."

Jane starts moving back and forth, patting her pockets, picking up boxes like she's looking for something.

"It's OK. We've done nothing wrong," I say, approaching her slowly.

She backs away and sits down heavily on the sofa, her eyes fixed straight ahead at the dark, rectangular hole in the floor. She takes a long, deep breath.

"How about we bury it somewhere?" she begins quietly. "Let's just wrap it up and take it to…" she searches for the words, "…to the fields. One night. We bury it properly, in the ground." Her confidence is returning, her voice gaining assurance. "We forget it."

She looks at me, composed once again, legs apart, elbows on her knees. "In two or three years' time, this place will be worth at least twice as much, we'll sell up, we'll move on. We can go wherever then, I could set up in a pub somewhere, get a Michelin star, we can move out. To the Cotswolds or wherever."

I look at her with disbelief. She's not thinking straight. "Whoever did this was desperate," I say. "We've disturbed a grave. Where's your compassion?"

"I don't want people knowing about this."

"This is someone's baby!"

"I don't want to know." She looks at the ground.

"You're not curious how it got here?"

"We had all these plans, and then the first thing we do… we find this. It's fucked." She hangs her head in her hands. "It's ruined everything."

"You can't blame this."

Her fingers tense on her scalp.

"Things haven't been right for a long time," I say quietly.

She looks to me, her glazed eyes full of contempt. I look at the baby. New life, new beginnings. This one a petrified husk.

"I'm not happy," I say.

137

"Oh, Tam, please." She deflates into the sofa cushions. "What do you feel?" she asks sharply. "Sadness? You're fucking depressed!"

"What would you know, you're barely here."

"I do my best. I'm doing my best."

The coffee pot screams, steam pouring from its spout, a burning smell filling the flat.

"Fuck!" Jane runs across the room and grabs the handle, yelling, "Jesus, hot!", as she turns the burner off with the other hand. She throws the whole thing into the sink, wet black grains splattering across the tiles.

"It's OK," I say again, coming over to her. I reach for her burnt hand. She relents, and I run it under the tap, turning it slowly in mine under the cold water.

"I don't know what to do, but we can't forget this. We can't avoid it. Some things need to be confronted."

She doesn't say anything, her gaze fixed on our hands and the stream running down the plughole. I look out across the fields, the grass studded with red poppies and blue cornflowers. They've surged for the sun and found the light. I knew I had felt something here. In my gut, while everyone else slept. The building had been trying to speak to me. Things not meant to be buried would always resurface.

"So much history," I say tentatively.

"What does that mean?"

"All of it. Us. This." I gesture at the boxes of stuff, the bundle on the counter.

She drops her hand from mine and turns away. "It feels like a bad dream."

"You can't be happy either."

"I feel like I can't reach you. Like everything I say makes it worse."

I sit on a stool. "It doesn't matter now."

For a minute we don't say anything. I feel my heart beating heavy in my chest.

She turns to face me. "Wait, why?"

I shrug. A sinking feeling in my stomach. "I think I should leave."

"You can't leave." She flaps her arms. "What about all this stuff?"

"I don't want it," I snap.

"Well, I'm not dealing with it!" she shouts.

I stand up. "There's no use talking now. We can work that out later."

"No, wait," she says, grabbing my shoulders, the desperate look returning to her eyes. "I think we should just put it back. Look." With carefully pinching fingers, she begins folding the rags back over the baby, retching as she brushes the skin of its exposed belly.

I grab her wrists and pull them down by her sides. I can feel her blood pulsing under my fingers. "Stop." Her eyes are tightly closed, a sob rising in her chest. I bring her close and the tension in her body dissipates. She sighs, letting her head fall on my shoulder.

Eventually, we separate, my dressing gown wet with her tears. I turn towards the baby. The rags are stiff between my fingers. I can't wrap the baby up the same way again, but I do my best to cover its body, to be respectful. "I'm going to get my phone so we can report this," I say, turning towards the stairs. As I reach the first step, I hear the front door close. She's gone.

Bones are levers to be acted upon by muscles. They are protective cases for soft structures hanging in a divine arrangement of columns, cavities and extremities. They vary greatly in construction. In the form and structure of apparently unmeaning bone mass, there exists provisions for working; a power whose nature remains elusive. Bones are storage devices, holding fats and minerals for distribution; they always remember.

16 September 1975

First, they dunk the fillets, sometimes three times, their
fingers pinching the tail end firmly as it's removed, excess
batter sliding back into the bucket. Connie likes to watch
them fry the fish; the fillets tremble as though electrified by
the hot fat. Fish and chips for one might be a lonely dinner,
but Connie prefers it to cooking alone. She likes getting out
of the studios these days. The surrounding streets have
familiar faces now and the chippy is a good place to think.
She has her pick of the empty booths, and she shuffles into
one of them, the back of her legs squeaking on the
leatherette. She plonks her sweating parcel on the Formica
table. The fluorescent light flickers. She unzips her jacket and
pulls it off her shoulders as clouds of steam from the fryer
plume upwards, giving everything a greasy sheen.

Kieran's departure seemed to shock no-one. People
shrugged; artists were coming and going all the time. Least
surprised of all was Pamela—she'd just shaken her head and
said, "I warned you not to let him get to you." Connie's
protests had been futile, with Pamela cutting her short and
refusing to talk about it any further. She feels ashamed, as
though she's let Pamela down. Still, she can't let it drop. She
knows she's missed something. She keeps thinking about the
party, and afterwards in her flat. About his anger. There has
to be more to it.

The studio has revealed no clues. Nothing. She'd gone
back up a few times. Spotless. She'd called Fred, the studio
manager, at his home address in Putney, straining to hear
over the roar of the busses outside. He was annoyed to be
bothered on the weekend but told her not to worry. He said
Kieran had settled his rent a month in advance; he said they'd
fill the studio in no time—in fact, a friend of his son's was

interested. *Awfully nice bloke.* Would she mind showing him around? *Thanks muchly.* When she explained that it was already spotless and said wasn't that a bit fishy, he'd said, "No, no. Saves you a job, doesn't it, then, dear? Toodle-oo!" and put the phone down, leaving her standing there, dial tone ringing in her ear.

She unpeels the outer layers of newsprint, the type still legible, before rolling the parcel over to find the next pages translucent with grease, the softened paper tearing easily between her fingers. Good riddance to him. The only person who wanted to talk to her about it was Jim. They'd managed to work through the falling out over his dust project; something had shifted between them in her room that night. Were they friends? They shared something now; he'd seen the look in Kieran's eyes too. It still makes the hair on the back of her neck stand on end.

She stares out of the windows, their big glass panes fogged up with steam. She pulls out the notepad she started almost a year ago, just before she moved in. Each page is crammed with her scrawled writing; lists upon lists, dates and names and sums. She'll be needing to get a new one soon. Time to make some changes. She needs to remember what Pamela said all those months ago: stop separating the art from life, the office from the studio. It's all systems and structures. Starving, she peels back the last layer of newspaper, the fish and chips steaming. A liberal shake of salt. A drenching of vinegar. She always asks for wrapped because they give you more. Stabbing the crispy batter of the fish with a wooden fork, she lifts rubbery, hot flakes into her mouth before reaching for a bottle of sauce and shaking out a big brown blob onto the newspaper. She looks through her notes; if only she could figure out where he'd gone. Perhaps there is a detail she's recorded that might jog a forgotten memory.

Two street cleaners park their brush trolleys outside and pull woollen hats from their grimy faces as they enter the shop. Connie pushes away her dinner and sinks back into the banquette. Stuffed. She closes her notepad. The Open Studios exhibition was finally here—only two more weeks to go. She needs to focus. One last push. This Kieran business has been a distraction; it's time to show the artists at Tower Street who she really is. A handful of chips lie scattered across the paper. She thinks about evenings in Crawley, with everyone crammed around the electric fire in Nan's front room watching *The Generation Game*. A pang of guilt. She hasn't seen them in months. Her eyes drift over the newspaper, stomach distended. She reads the first few words of a narrow column partially obscured by splodges of brown sauce: "Hackney Girl Bleeds to Death on Bus". Connie leans forward and reads.

> Hotel maid Mrs Smith was making her way home to Bromley-by-Bow after dinner service when she witnessed the terrible ordeal. "She was collapsed on the floor of the top deck, poor child. Oh, it was awful. She passed away right there in my arms. I'm still very upset by it all, you know—things are getting worse these days. The youth. It's not right."

The text continues, rendered unreadable by her stabbing chip fork. Underneath is a photograph—a school portrait of a girl with long hair, a pale round face and pretty almond eyes. Her head is cocked slightly to one side. That's odd... Connie recognises her. A grey soaked skirt drifts into her mind. The girl in the rain. Underneath the photo the caption reads: "Brenda Warren, 15, of Barnet Grove, Bethnal Green". It's her! She sits up quickly, knocking chips off the table.

Those who suffer have limited options: die, survive or recover. Acute infections are rapid kinds of diseases, and it's rare for their handiwork to reach bone: death arrives first. Meanwhile, a chronic infection lasts, recurring once or many times over a long period, even a lifetime. The basic response to an attack of pathogens is inflammation: a process of pain, heat, redness and swelling. Inflammation can lead to skeletal changes, from pitting of the bone surface to the growth of disorganised woven bone and compact bone. Shadows appear on X-rays. In severe cases of infection, new bone can form around dead bone like a rotten toffee apple. The bottom line: bone persists in whatever way it can.

14 October 1974, three hundred and thirty-four days before the Night

The lip gloss label reads "Kissing Potion". It's the colour of shiny new copper. Sitting amongst eye shimmer and powdery blush, the lip gloss sparkles in its little glass roller applicator. The girl watches two shop assistants in white tunics assemble the display; "Promise Richie Your Raspberry Kisses" is the campaign slogan. Peeking through gaps in between bottles of shampoo, she watches their candyfloss hair bobbing as they bend to unpack boxes, arranging the products into attractive clusters. "Orange Crush" was the one she wanted—it would have gone nicely with her hair—but it's sold out. Kissing Potion would do.

The gloss smells sweet like marzipan. She rolls the hard little ball over her lips, and her nose twitches; she sniffles. It tickles!

Brenda is 14, but she's tall for her age so thinks she's older. An early bloomer, her mum says. Some people say she's flighty, which she likes; others say bolshy, which she doesn't. Deep down, she doesn't care what they say. She just lifts her dimpled chin in defiance. "They're jealous," her mum says. Remember: sticks and stones. She has to wear her uniform in the evenings after school because her parents can only afford one set of clothes and they're for best. So she folds her dowdy old blazer into her satchel and hitches her skirt up. She does alright with what she's got.

Brenda goes out whenever she can. She hates being home, with its cramped, chintzy rooms and her frightened mum. She wanders around Bethnal Green after school, sometimes walking with no destination at all, just following her nose. She knows all the short cuts, the fences with holes in; which curtains twitch, which dogs bark. She likes to sit on the benches in London Fields and dream about being an air hostess. "A trolley dolly," her mum says disparagingly. She just ignores her.

"That's not your colour, dear," an assistant says, pointing at Kissing Potion.

Brenda shrugs and pretends to return it to the shelf, slipping it down the sleeve of her blouse instead. She lingers at the Revlon counter, touching as many tubes as she can, testing them out until the back of her hand shimmers like a peacock's tail. Over at the till, the shop assistants eye her uneasily. She heads to the perfume rack, squirts Charlie Blue across her blouse and with a flick of her hair, and her most insincere smile, she turns and exits the shop.

On the street outside the market, sellers count notes and load vans. In less than twelve hours they'll be back, unpacking everything again. How boring. What a life! Day after day in this horrid place; just imagine. Not for her, no way. She's getting out.

She first sees him shouldering through the men waving betting stubs outside the bookmakers. Their pink balding heads a sea of thumbs. All that shouting. Maybe it's his hair that draws her in: thick and curly; a deep brown, the colour of chestnuts; long, like the boys on *Top of the Pops*. Maybe it's his jeans: stone-washed, flared below the knee, tight around his bum. Maybe it's his walk: hips forward, snaking. She swears the old dears clutch their pearls as he passes. A camera swings from his neck like he's a fashion photographer or a reporter. He's famous-looking, fearless. Before she can think twice, she's following him. She can hear his heels clip against the pavement. She likes his boots; imagines them set down neatly in the hall next to her mum's flat pumps and her own patent leather lace-ups.

He turns right and disappears, heading north towards Hackney. She has to rush to keep pace with his loping gait. She reaches the corner fewer than ten paces behind. Maybe he lives in the squats around the fields. "Hippies need to get proper jobs," her mum says. The workday is ending. Traffic shunts forward nose-to-tail, brakes squeaking. The shops thin out and so do the people. The pavement widens. She slows down. Exposed. She follows him past the railway arches; past the shell of a car, its parts splayed on the floor around its body. Three men in grubby overalls drink mugs of tea, their faces black with grease and the pinks of their mouths glistening wet.

By the canal, he turns down Andrews Road, uphill towards Broadway Market. She's relieved he hasn't gone down to the towpath. She avoids the canal: no lights. It's a place for rats and stinking barges, all full of rubbish. She watches his jeans crease as he walks. She feels his rhythm feeding her own and imagines what it would be like to kiss him. She slips the lip-gloss roller out of her sleeve and re-applies it thickly.

For a moment she worries she's lost him—this route is unfamiliar. Then he's there, walking to the left of London Fields, towards Trederwen Road and streets her mum has warned her about: "Do not go down there! Never!" Full of grimy, brick houses. Squats and squatters, hippies, deviants, drunks and druggies, low-down dirty families kicked out of other places. The vacant terraces were "like broken teeth in a healthy mouth", her mum had said. Rows and rows of them. Some of their windows and doors are bricked up; others have scorched boards and hoarding, corrugated metal nailed over them. She steals herself, turning to look back. Past the green lies the railway line, the grocer's, the Queen's Head, and then her own little bedroom with its purple sheets and cream walls. She is further out of her territory with each nervous step.

No people to see now. No cars, no dogs, no washing lines fluttering. No windows! At the end of the street, there's a pile of broken furniture and rubber tyres. Footprints trail mud all over. The street hasn't a cut through, just a walled dead end. It's like he's vanished. Her mouth is dry, sickly with the fake orange flavour of the lip gloss. He must be inside one of the houses. Is he watching her? She smooths down her hair, tilts her head, stands up tall. She looks towards the entrance of one of the houses, its doorway in shadow. The corrugated metal sheeting has been peeled back like a scab. She knows she should turn back but an exhilarated spirit has possessed her, and she walks up the path towards the door. The weeds come up to her waist. She steps inside. The narrow corridor is dark, but slowly, a familiar layout reveals itself. It's just like her mum's. Downstairs: a front room and kitchen. Upstairs: a few bedrooms, and maybe a bathroom if the previous tenants were lucky. The air has an earthy smell, but something else too. Tobacco. A wave of heat rushes to her cheeks. The light that spills past the dislodged metal sheeting illuminates the first few steps of the staircase; the rest stays in shadow. He is close. She can sense it.

"Have you been following me?" His voice is quiet and deliberate, slicing through the dank air that separates them. A deep voice—a voice she wants to swallow; to be in her ears and mouth. Despite the slight tremble in her legs, she steps forward without a falter, and her green eyes, having adjusted to the gloom, see the toes of his boots.

Afterword

In the early 1970s artists in London worked together to create studio organisations in former industrial buildings. In the decades since, the roles artists have played within gentrification have been well-documented by academics, journalists, and in popular culture. However, women administrators, often pivotal figures in these organisations' infrastructure, and the impact of their work have been largely ignored.

Although *Innominate* is a work of fiction and the events it depicts did not happen, I wrote the book to address this absence.

From 2016–2020, I conducted interviews with artists and administrators who lived and worked in studio buildings over the last fifty years. I drew these conversations into conflict with my own recent experiences as a studio administrator, rearranging space and time to construct the story you've just read. Its main protagonist, Connie, is therefore a composite character. She never existed and yet her struggles are real.

Often, the women I interviewed expressed their fear of having lived a life which didn't make sense or, as photographer and studio caretaker Shirley Read put it, having a career that "didn't add up". I wanted the fusing together of our stories to operate as an act of collective defiance, a tribute to the (many) unknown women administrators whose activities remain unaccounted for.

Writer Alice Hattrick told me once that "finding and discovering are acts of desire". In regard to this book, the historical source which first sparked my yearning was a short documentary commissioned in 1970 by the studio organisation SPACE. Directed by Peter Montagnon, the film features artists at St Katharine Docks, including interviews with SPACE founders Bridget Riley and Peter Sedgley, and footage of the Art Information Registry (AIR).

In my pursuit of the past, I consulted meeting minutes, newspaper articles, correspondence, photographs and maps held at SPACE, the British Library, Camden Local Studies and Archive Centre, Hackney Archives, Matt's Gallery and the Women's Art Library at Goldsmiths, University of London. These archives, as well as the personal collections of Robin Klassnik, Letty Mooring and Shirley Read, have helped me to bring artist studio life and seventies Hackney to the page.

My mother grew up poor in London, her childhood memories, fears, aspirations and disappointments have shaped this book in more ways than I know.

Alongside these witnesses, I listened to the studio buildings themselves. Sometimes they no longer existed. Even so, I travelled across the city to these sites, spending time walking, sitting and writing field notes. My approach was attuned by writer Maria Fusco's method of trying to "act as a recording device": a process that resists evaluation in favour of description, operating as a bundle of senses and destabilising the privileging of sight by absorbing smell, sound, touch and taste.

Site-writing in a teaching mortuary in Scotland informed the "bone index" that, like a spine, connects the multiple timelines of this story. The six months I spent observing cadaveric dissections reshaped how I thought about architecture, its remodelling and mortality. What kind of body is the artist studio, I wondered, how does it bear weight, provide support? When does it break?

Innominate traces the collective afterlife of these contacts, transformed into fictional narrative.

What can fiction do? Fiction doesn't force its sources to go public; it accommodates multiple points of view, the human and the nonhuman; it lets bricks speak. Fiction

153

encourages complex, complicit characters, shifting between the intimate and the procedural. It can tell you what she's thinking. It can make the bad guys pay. Or not. Maybe they never do. Fiction might be the only retribution available. Fiction feels able to bear the weight of my demands for history to have been different.

Acknowledgements

Thank you to Anna Bunting-Branch, Lauren Craig, Philip Ewe, Laura Guy, Matthew Harle, Alice Hattrick, Matthew McQuillan, Stuart Middleton, Gina Nembhard, Jenny Pearce, Charlie Prodger, Sarah Stott, Isabelle Sully and Ed Webb-Ingall for their wisdom and encouragement.

I am in debt to my parents for the opportunities afforded by their sacrifices; my fearless and enthusiastic editor, Susan Finlay at MOIST; as well as Phoebe Blatton and Maddy Hamey-Thomas, for their insightful notes and proofreading throughout the production process.

The financial support of the Scottish Graduate School for Arts & Humanities (SGSAH) made it possible for me to undertake a practice-based PhD at the University of Edinburgh, during which an early version of this book was developed, shepherded by my tireless supervisors Maria Fusco, Elizabeth Reeder and Rebecca Collins. Zoë Strachan and the students in the creative writing workshop at the University of Glasgow (2016–2017) were my first readers and I am grateful for their kindness. Professor Sue Black and Dr Craig Cunningham at the Centre for Anatomy and Human Identification (CAHID), University of Dundee, shared their knowledge of osteology and forensic anthropology with enthusiasm and generosity, thank you.

To the administrators and archivists who maintain the libraries and collections I visited during the writing of this book: thank you for your diligence and care. I am particularly appreciative of Althea Greenan at the Women's Art Library, Goldsmiths, University of London, whose commitment and openness keeps feminist lives accessible for those of us who follow in their footsteps to find.

I was fortunate to call upon the memories and reflections of Paul Carter, Mary Hurrell, Robin Klassnik, Peter Sedgley and James Faure Walker, all of whom were kind enough to share their experiences of artist studios in London from the 1970s to the present day. To all the artists involved with the Woodmill in Bermondsey from 2009–2016, without your energy and risk taking, this book would not exist.

Conversations with Chris McCormack, Anna Harding and Ego Ahaiwe Sowinski set me on course: thank you for introducing me to Letty Mooring, Shirley Read and Rita Keegan. My deepest gratitude goes to these three women. You welcomed me into your homes, shared your stories and answered my questions with grace. I cherish our conversations; thank you for your record keeping, for your creativity and resilience.

About the Author

Naomi Pearce is a writer and curator. Recent exhibitions include *Almost Conceptual*, Matt's Gallery, and *56 Artillery Lane*, Raven Row (co-curated with Amy Budd), both in London. Her writing has been published by Art Monthly, Happy Hypocrite, e-flux Criticism, Kunstverein Munich, and The White Review, among others. From 2018–2022 she was a member of the Rita Keegan Archive Project, a social history and curatorial collective, whose recent activity includes an exhibition at the South London Gallery and the publication *Mirror Reflecting Darkly* with MIT Press. *Innominate* is her first novel.

Innominate is the second book in MOIST's third season. The other titles in "Body of Evidence" are:

Know Thy Audience by Nadia de Vries
Silicone God by Victoria Brooks